CHARLIE DICK

CHARLIE DICK

by *Laura Fisher*
illustrated by Rocco Negri

HOLT, RINEHART AND WINSTON
New York · Chicago · San Francisco

Books by Laura Fisher

CHARLIE DICK

NEVER TRY NATHANIEL

YOU WERE PRINCESS LAST TIME

AMY AND THE SORREL SUMMER

for Eric

1

With his dirty thumbnail Charlie Dick tested the clothespin trigger he had just fastened to the carved wooden pistol. His tanned face broke into a grin as the clothespin snapped shut in good form.

"I'm probably the best clothespin-gun maker in all Wyoming," he complimented himself.

Because of the Depression, ready-made guns were hard to come by, but his pride in his creation made him more pleased than if the gun had been ordered from the 1938 Sears catalogue. He stooped to the coalshed floor and with Mama's scissors cut a round strip from a discarded tire tube, then dexterously fitted it over the end of his pistol, pinching it into the clothespin.

After peeking around the coalshed doorway, cautiously, with pistol ready, he crept along the weed-lined path near the side of the old brown house. At the corner Charlie

Dick paused and pushed the blond hair out of his eyes. He carefully surveyed the yard and the clotheslines and the weathered kitchen door that opened on them, hoping to see one of his four sisters—Miriam, Anna, Kathleen, or Elizabeth Eliza. Suddenly the door flew open. He drew back and pressed his body against the wall.

"Charles Richard Hale!" called Miriam, his older sister. "Charles Richard Hale," she called again louder, "Mama wants you right now."

There's a target that will make a lot of noise when it's hit, Charlie Dick thought as he slid the point of his gun around the corner. Miriam was already turning back into the kitchen, leaving the door open.

"He doesn't answer, Mama. I sure don't know where he's gone."

From inside the house the crying of baby Elizabeth Eliza didn't drown out the rhythmic sloshing of the old washing machine.

"I was too slow," Charlie Dick whispered, blinking his blue eyes in annoyance at himself, "but I'll be ready next time."

And he was when Miriam again came outside a moment later. Her spindly twelve-year-old body was hardly able to carry the basket of wet clothes to be hung to dry. Charlie Dick's homemade weapon followed her progress past the two big cottonwoods to the clothesline. Miriam, ungainly as a sagebrush limb, leaned over the basket. Her brown stringy hair flopped forward across her narrow

2

shoulders as she pulled out the damp dish towels and draped them over her arm. Charlie Dick's thumb slowly pressed the clothespin trigger. Miriam's howl was just like he knew it would be—loud. In addition she jumped high in the air, spilling the dish towels off her arm into the dirt. Her scream turned into an angry threat as she ran to the house.

"Charlie Dick, I'll tell Mama on you. Mama, Charlie Dick's out here."

Charlie Dick darted back along the little path, but he was still in sight when his mother at the corner called, "Charlie Dick, you come in here this very minute. You know we've been looking for you all morning."

"Doggone it," he complained to himself as he stuffed his gun inside the front of his overalls and turned back. He had hoped to get in a couple more shots before he was caught and put to work, but Miriam was the biggest tattle-tale in all Hanging Rock Valley. She always ruined everything. He stepped into the kitchen.

"Charlie Dick shot me when I was bent over. Oh, it hurts, and he made me drop the clean dish towels and get them dirty," Miriam smugly told Mama.

"For heaven's sake, Charlie Dick. Do you have to make mischief on a day like today?" asked Margaret Hale. "Today when I've got so much to do." She smoothed her disordered hair back from her eyes.

"And Charlie Dick's gone and made another rubber gun," Miriam prodded Mama, hopeful of some punishment for her adversary.

4

"I've told you a thousand times not to use my clothespins for your old guns." Mama felt the lump in the bib of his overalls, then crossly pulled out the weapon.

"But that's the best gun I ever made," Charlie Dick complained as his mother pulled off the clothespin and tossed it into the clothes basket. "You didn't have to break it up." To show Miriam whose fault it was, he bulged his eyes out at her. She sniffed loudly with injured dignity.

"I won't have any more of this, Charlie Dick," Margaret Hale scolded her son. "Not one more of your tricks. You know we need your help, but you just cause us more work. Now Miriam will have to rinse out those clothes again that you made her drop on the ground. You're to come right upstairs with me and help me move the good bed to the downstairs bedroom so we can have it ready for Grandpa by the time Daddy brings him home."

"I don't mind moving the mattress," Charlie Dick told his mother as she dropped another batch of clothes into the old washing machine, "but I hate to make beds. I won't have to help make beds, will I? That's a girl's job."

"Charlie Dick," his mother said tiredly as they left the kitchen, "you'll just have to do what we need done today whether it's to your liking or not."

He unwillingly followed her up the old staircase. He wished that his father were home and that he were out helping him now as he had been almost every day for the week since school was out.

One day they had fenced. Dad had driven the bull

from the small pasture into the stackyard. Then together they put in several new posts and tightened the wires of the pasture fence.

"Things will be better this year," John Hale said as he shoveled the dirt into the posthole. That's how grownups talked about the Depression, and Charlie Dick was pleased to have his father speak to him as he would another adult. The boy tightened his hold on the cedar post to keep it perfectly in place while Dad tamped the earth down around it.

"This year we should get something for our crops for a change," John Hale continued. "That's why this spring I've planted all the land. It'll be extra work, Charlie Dick, a lot more than I can do. A ten-year-old like you can be a lot of help, so if things work out, maybe we can see about giving you something, a few dollars, kind of wages, like you've been asking for." That's what his father had told him only a few days ago. Now today what was Charlie Dick's mother asking him to do? Make beds. A girl's job!

At the top of the stairs six-year-old Kathleen was tugging a sheet from a pile of quilts that had been pulled from the beds. As he passed, Charlie Dick twisted her blond braid and bared his teeth in a horrible grimace that only he could effect.

"Mama, Mama," Kathleen wailed, running around Charlie Dick to her mother.

"What in the world is the matter?" Margaret Hale asked.

Kathleen clung to her skirt, howling. "Charlie Dick's been smiling at me again."

Charlie Dick dabbed half-heartedly at the streaks of vinegar water he had sloshed on the downstairs bedroom window.

"That's clean enough," he said to himself, dropping his wipe cloth to the floor.

He tugged the heavy window open, picked up his pail and threw the water out through the screen. Then, gathering the rags into the pail, he walked from the bedroom.

Anna sat by the baby, Elizabeth Eliza, on the floor in the living room, but they made no commotion, so Charlie Dick walked almost all the way through the room before he realized that something was not right. He stopped in his tracks.

"Anna?"

No sound came from his fragile eight-year-old sister, but her thin body sagged as though weighed down by a sack of chicken feed.

"Anna, what's . . . ?" Charlie Dick broke off abruptly.

Torn bits of cardboard were scattered in all directions from Elizabeth Eliza's lap, and saliva dripped from a sewing spool in her mouth.

Anna's little hand futilely gathered at the mutilated fragments of the precious miniature doll furniture that she had so laboriously cut from cardboard, glued onto spools, and painted with shoe polish and cherry juice. From under her long dark hair, silent tears dropped onto the torn bits.

"Elizabeth Eliza!" Charlie Dick scolded. He grabbed the spool from the toddler's mouth.

"Mine." She reached to take it back.

"No, no, no."

The baby howled, her face contorted by her offended feelings.

Miriam trotted in from the kitchen. "Charlie Dick, you stop making Elizabeth Eliza cry. Did you hurt her?"

"I didn't do nothing to Elizabeth Eliza," Charlie Dick angrily countered Miriam, who always accused him falsely. He stooped down and began collecting the scattered spools. He spoke confidently to Anna. "I bet we can fix it."

Anna shook her head. "No, it's all ruined."

"No, it's not, Anna. See, this chair would just need a new back." He pressed the broken chair into Anna's hand.

"Oh!" shrieked Miriam, just now realizing what had happened. She jumped around on her gangly legs. "Oh, look what Elizabeth Eliza has done to Anna's doll furniture."

At Miriam's outburst the rest of the family collected around the girls on the floor. Above the confusion Miriam still moaned, "Poor Anna. Oh, poor Anna, and she worked so long to make it."

In the kitchen a few minutes later Charlie Dick scooted along the bench to his place at the table next to Anna. His mother with Elizabeth Eliza in one arm gathered the folded, clean laundry from the table. She set an enamel pitcher of milk and a plate of homemade bread in the middle of the oilcloth.

"You ain't still crying, Anna?" Charlie Dick whispered.

Anna didn't answer, but one lone tear slid from her dark, solemn eyes and rolled down her cheek. It was always Anna's sad eyes that got Charlie Dick.

"I'll help you fix up your doll furniture. I will tomorrow, Anna. It'll be just like new."

If Anna were a tattletale like Miriam or a crybaby like Kathleen, Charlie Dick wouldn't care a mite for her troubles, but her forlorn, silent tears were too much.

"It might even be better than it was before Elizabeth Eliza got into your box and tore it all up. Yes, it will. It will be a hundred times better with me helping you make it."

"Elizabeth Eliza is too little to know any better," Mama tried to comfort as she poured milk in the bowls for the children.

"I keep my things up high so she can't get them," Kathleen untactfully told everyone.

Anna's tears kept quietly flowing as she broke some bread into the bowl of milk.

Charlie Dick leaned over and whispered in her ear.

"And if you don't cry any more, I'll get you a doll just the size of the furniture to go with it," he promised rashly. He tucked the doll away at the bottom of his mental list that included BB guns and pocketknives, the list that had begun when Dad relented to Charlie Dick's coaxing for wages.

The tears stopped, and Anna began eating her bread and milk. Charlie Dick decided she must be feeling better, and he felt better too.

"It's sure good to have our housework finished," said Miriam. "We won't have to work so hard tomorrow, will we?"

"I don't know." Mama was feeding Elizabeth Eliza her dinner. "It will be more work with Grandpa here. You'll all have to help me."

"Anyway we won't have to clean out the windows next to the screens tomorrow. That was awful today," Miriam said, "with all those dead flies in them."

"Don't talk about flies when we're eating." Kathleen covered her mouth as though she suddenly had an upset stomach.

Charlie Dick poured a second bowl of milk. He smiled to himself as he broke a large slice of bread into it. "I ate a fly once."

"Charlie Dick, you did not," Miriam scoffed.

Kathleen clapped her hands over her ears.

"Yes, I did." He shoveled a heaping spoonful of the soggy bread into his mouth. "You see, I was running after

Dan Barns in Hanging Rock, and I had my mouth open and it flew right in."

"Charlie Dick, don't start any more of your teases now," his tired mother warned.

But Charlie Dick continued, "That fly went straight down into my belly without even touching a tonsil."

"I couldn't hear anything you said, Charlie Dick," argued Kathleen, removing her hands from her ears, "and anyway you just made that all up."

"It didn't taste so bad neither. They ain't so bad, are they, Anna?" Charlie Dick turned to the silent little Anna, hoping to draw her into his game, but she didn't nod in agreement as she usually did at whatever Charlie Dick asked her.

Miriam stared into her bowl. "I keep thinking I'm eating those dead flies."

Kathleen whimpered.

"Yes, I kinda like the taste of flies."

Kathleen let out a loud, despairing wail.

Miriam yelled, "Mama, make Charlie Dick stop."

Mama banged her hand down hard on the table. "I might as well talk to a cedar post as tell you anything, Charlie Dick. Stop right now." Mama half stood as she shook her finger at him. "Just one more tease and you'll leave the table." She sat back down. "We're all so tired."

"Doggone it, I was just having some fun."

"Charlie Dick is always mean teasing," Miriam accused. "He torments more than any boy I've ever seen."

Charlie Dick shoved a hunk of bread between his teeth and chewed noisily with his mouth open. He stretched his neck across the table toward his sisters. Miriam pulled the corners of her mouth down in a sour expression.

The sound of the pickup motor rumbled through the night air. Kathleen was the only one who hadn't eaten all her bread and milk, but the rest of the family jumped up, leaving her to finish alone. Margaret Hale handed Elizabeth Eliza to Miriam, and Anna touched her cheeks, still blotchy from crying, then ran from the kitchen to hide.

Charlie Dick threw open the door and peered out just as the lights of the pickup switched off.

"Son, come and carry in Grandpa's clothes," his father's voice called from the darkness.

"O.K.," was the boy's quick answer. He was glad to be the one in the family called to help. He ran through the weeds, following the light from the doorway out to the pickup.

"Hi, Grandpa," he sang out to the open truck door as he reached his father.

No answer came from inside the cab.

Dad gave him a cardboard box before he turned to the pickup and lifted the old man from it. Carrying the box, Charlie Dick followed his father to the house.

With the exception of Anna, who was nowhere in sight, the whole family accompanied Dad into the downstairs bedroom. Charlie Dick put the box on the floor then pushed between Kathleen and Miriam to stand next to the bed where Dad had laid his old father. Charles

Hale looked as helpless as a bundle of gunnysacks. Mama pulled a patchwork quilt up over his thin frame.

"You children say hello to Grandpa, then move on out of here," was Dad's order. "Grandpa's tired from the trip and doesn't need you all standing around bothering him."

The girls dutifully chorused, "Hello, Grandpa."

From under shaggy, gray brows the old man glared up at them with eyes the color of faded denim.

Mama leaned down and kissed the wrinkled forehead before turning away. "I'll get you some bread and milk."

When the others were leaving the bedroom, Charlie Dick walked closer to the bed.

"You didn't bring your big pocketknife with you, did you? The one with the black handle and five blades? I'll get it out of your box for you if you want."

A fire smoldered under Grandpa Hale's eyebrows. "Why would I bring that? I'm through with anything that has any doing in this world. All I've got left is others doing for me." The weathered lips snapped shut into a solid line.

"Charlie Dick, come away and stop bothering Grandpa," Dad's voice was stern.

The boy spun around and rushed from the bedroom back to the kitchen, where Mama was breaking some bread into a clean bowl. "Oh, John, he's so thin." she said.

Dad sat on the end of the bench near the table and pulled his hat from his head. The deep tan of his face contrasted with the white of his forehead.

"I stopped by Dr. Ryan's with him on the way out. He's worse than we thought. We should have brought him here sooner. But I don't know how you're going to manage even now."

"I don't know how you're going to manage," was Mama's reply. "I just don't—with so much work on the summer crops and no help to be hired in this whole country for love or money."

"But I'm going to help Daddy this summer," Charlie Dick loudly corrected his mother, who didn't pay the least attention.

Even his father ignored the comment. "And we'll need some cash for medicine for Grandpa too."

"I sure wish Grandpa had brought his big black pocketknife with the can opener on it," Charlie Dick complained.

"And Charlie Dick," Dad pointed his large, rough finger at his son, "none of your tricks on Grandpa. Do you hear? None! We're going to have to have more cooperation all the way around. You get into bed now."

Charlie Dick went out the back door and along the short board sidewalk into the dark porch. He liked having the concrete porch for his very own sleeping room. It was enclosed by three rough wooden walls and a roof. The fourth side was mostly screen, and he had pushed his cot near where he could watch for falling stars in the dark sky and hear the cautious rustlings of night. Sometimes toward morning when it was pretty cool, he would kick the heavy quilt off just to prove nothing was too cold for him. Now he plopped down on his cot and stared out at the myriad tiny lights in the sky.

"He didn't bring his big pocketknife, and he's even grumpier than ever," Charlie Dick mused aloud to himself.

A stirring in the porch made him swing to a sitting position. He wondered if one of the half-wild cats from the barn had crawled back there to sleep. Slowly as his eyes became accustomed to the blackness, he made out large eyes shining from a pale face.

"I thought you was a cat, Anna." He didn't even admit to himself that the unexpected movement had given him a fright. "What are you doing here?" He was glad it was Anna rather than any of his other sisters.

Anna didn't answer but glided through the darkness and sat next to her brother on the cot.

"You don't need to hide from Grandpa, Anna," Charlie Dick advised the quiet girl. "You lived here first, you know."

After a moment of silence Anna asked, "Will it have golden hair?"

"Will what?" Charlie Dick was puzzled.

"The tiny doll for my furniture."

"Oh! Sure it will, Anna. Sure it will," Charlie Dick passed over the doll quickly, "and tomorrow we'll fix that furniture all back up better than new. How would you like that?" He grinned at his little sister, and although he couldn't be sure because it was so dark, he thought she smiled back.

2

Charlie Dick wriggled uncomfortably on the hard wooden chair in the corner of the downstairs bedroom. If only Grandpa had brought his big five-blade pocketknife, then somehow Charlie Dick could manage to prop it on top of the clothes in the box and have it to look at from a distance. Although just looking might wear thin for the long hour in which he was required to sit with Grandpa, at least it would be something to do.

"We don't want Grandpa to get lonesome or feel unwanted," his mother had instructed the children the day after he came. "One of you can sit with him each morning." This morning Mama assigned Charlie Dick the job. "Since it's too wet to mow today, you sit with Grandpa so the girls can help me."

"But Daddy will need me anyway."

"I'm going to do some ditching," John Hale said, "and

that's a one-man job, so you help your mother today."
After breakfast Dad had gone off alone to the east field to
clean out the irrigation ditch.

Now Charlie Dick sighed as he squirmed. He pulled
his bare feet up on the chair and rested his chin on his
knee through the hole in his striped bib overalls.

The old man suddenly turned his head toward the boy.
"Your dad started the first crop yet?" Charles Hale demanded in his graty voice.

"He sharpened the mower blades this morning while I
drove Buttons and the other cows over to the pasture. I
would have started the mowing if it wasn't so wet, but it
rained last night." Charlie Dick wiggled his bare toes up
and down three times.

"Well, he'd better get started or he won't get no third
crop of hay at all." Grandpa's head swung back straight
and he lay staring up at the ceiling, his skin the color of
the ash heap behind the coalshed.

"I'm going to do most of the mowing and raking this
year," Charlie Dick bragged. "Dad said he'd pay me
wages. I'm the hired man."

Grandpa lay silent, unimpressed, only flicking his
white eyelashes once in a while. Then the eyelids closed
and he said as though in a dream, "John Cross got the
first derrick fork in all Hanging Rock Valley. I was about
seventeen and me and my pa went over to see it. He
showed us how he pushed it into the hay to load it, but
he didn't have his horse hitched to it to let us see how the

fork would lift over the haystack and dump the hay, so I got hold of the big rope and pulled the fork from the hayrack to the stack. 'Strong as a horse,' they all said . . ." Grandpa's voice trailed off.

"Really, Grandpa?" Charlie Dick exclaimed. "I'll bet I can do that. At least I'm gonna try. Every day I'll go over to the derrick and pull and pull, until I'm as strong as a horse."

But Grandpa wasn't listening. The heavy breathing from his partly open mouth told Charlie Dick that he had slipped off to sleep—maybe pulling up the loaded derrick fork in his dreams.

Charlie Dick put his legs down and nervously bounced in his chair. If Grandpa would only talk about old times like the derrick fork incident or the time when the Indians came or hunting bears on Bald Mountain, then it would be just dandy here with him, but he hardly ever did. He just lay there talking bitter or not saying anything at all. And that was no fun.

The heavy breathing turned into a snore, and the quilt near his face trembled from its force. Charlie Dick slid slowly from the chair, tiptoed to the door and moved silently into the disordered living room. His mother stood at the ironing board. Kathleen sat on a chair near her with the large mixing bowl in her lap. When she saw Charlie Dick sneaking from the bedroom, Margaret Hale frowned and pointed back to the door.

"But Grandpa's asleep," Charlie Dick spoke softly. "You can hear him snoring."

"Mama said *I* could scrape out the bowl she made Grandpa's birthday cake in," Kathleen said loudly. "You can't have any."

"I don't want any anyway, and be quiet or you'll wake Grandpa," Charlie Dick scolded softly.

"You do too want some. You're just saying that. Mama, don't let Charlie Dick grab my spoon," Kathleen bawled.

Grandpa's snores broke.

"Now see what you done, Kathleen. You woke Grandpa." Charlie Dick shook his fist at her.

But Mama took Charlie Dick's shoulder crossly and whispered in his ear, "Now go back in there and stay with Grandpa, and don't sneak off every time he closes his eyes. He'll think you don't want to be with him."

Muttering about Kathleen's loud voice, Charlie Dick trudged back to the bedroom and resumed his position on the chair.

Grandpa was awake with his white eyelashes blinking again, but he paid absolutely no attention to his grandson, who slumped on the chair and stared out the window at the inviting summer sky, which was the lovely blue shade of a magnesia bottle.

Then Grandpa was asleep again.

Charlie Dick just couldn't stand it—wasting a good morning, one of the few free from work, having no fun at all. He might as well be a dummy sitting on this chair for all Grandpa cared. Grandpa wouldn't even know the difference if he were only a laundry bag full of dirty clothes.

Suddenly Charlie Dick sat straight up and his eyes shot to the box of Grandpa's clothes. His lips stretched into a determined line. Cautiously he crept from the chair and moved toward the corner. He silently unsnapped the buckles on his bib overalls and pulled them off. Quickly he stuffed his pants and shirt with the clothes from Grandpa's box. A few seconds later he was cramming socks into a leg of a union suit that protruded from the opening of his shirt to make a head. With this quickly assembled dummy he tiptoed back to the chair.

Grandpa's snores were loud and steady when Charlie Dick in his underwear stepped back, tipped his head to one side consideringly, and broke into a wide grin.

Cautiously he crept to the door. The living room was empty. He ducked into the staircase and pulled a pair of Miriam's overalls from a nail there. After slipping them on and rolling up the pant legs, he streaked through the living room. He paused near the kitchen door to listen. When he determined that Mama and Kathleen were outside, he poked his head into the kitchen. On the table in front of the stack of unwashed dishes lay two round layers of white cake, cooling on a rack. Quickly Charlie Dick darted into the kitchen, broke himself a piece of cake, then dashed back through the living room and out the front door. He waited a moment, then dived around the side of the house into the shadow of the coalshed. With the shed to hide him from view, he sauntered leisurely, munching the cake and enjoying the warmth of the sun on his bare shoulders. At last he was free.

"I can't mow because of the rain, and Grandpa don't need me because he's asleep," he said to himself, "so this is just the time to put up a swing. That is, if I can find a rope."

A magpie flew from the open door of the toolshed before Charlie Dick ducked inside. He walked through the clutter of rusty mower blades and bent rivets over to the bridles and horse blankets that were tossed in disarray near the wall. After discovering two ropes, he chose the longest and on his way out picked up a board for the swing seat. As he crossed the yard, Miriam and Anna came out of the chicken coop. It had been Anna's turn to gather the eggs, but she was so frightened of some pecking hens that Mama had sent Miriam to poke the chickens from the nest for her.

"What are you doing with that rope and board, Charlie Dick?" Miriam sounded suspicious. "And you're supposed to be with Grandpa."

"He's asleep. So I'm going to make a swing."

"A swing?" Miriam beamed.

"A real one?" Anna's dark eyes shone.

"The best one ever made," Charlie Dick bragged. "It won't be just an ordinary tree swing. No sir. I'm gonna make it in the hayloft, and I'll swing so high I can look out the top of the barn and see all the way to Dan Barns's place." This, of course, was impossible, for Dan lived near Hanging Rock. Charlie Dick often wished Dan lived closer so he could have a boy to be with instead of just sisters.

"The swings you make in the cottonwoods by the house are always good ones," Anna suggested timidly.

"Not like this one. Why, swinging in this swing will be just like flying."

"It might go high, Charlie Dick, but it won't be like flying," Miriam contradicted, but she clasped her hands together and jumped around on her skinny legs, so Charlie Dick knew she was interested.

"And if you help me make it, I'll give you each a turn."

"But didn't Mama say we had to do the dishes, Miriam?" Anna worried.

"This won't take long," Charlie Dick said. He turned and strode off toward the barn.

"We could go for a minute, Anna," Miriam spoke from right behind Charlie Dick.

Anna, carrying her bucket of eggs, followed slowly.

In the horse barn Charlie Dick and Miriam climbed the wall ladder to the hayloft. Anna placed her bucket on the floor but stopped at the bottom of the ladder.

"Aren't you coming, Anna?" Miriam peered down from the edge of the loft.

"It's so high." Anna stood with her hand on the bottom rung.

"Oh, I'll help you, Anna," Miriam said impatiently.

She ungracefully scurried back down and standing behind Anna pushed her up the ladder. At the top Charlie

Dick helped pull her across the little space into the loft. After Anna was safely up, the frightened look faded from her face.

Charlie Dick shinnied up the hayloft's big center pole to the high beams halfway to the pointed roof. "Miriam, toss me up that rope."

After several unsuccessful attempts, Miriam threw the rope where he could catch it. He scooted along the cross-beam and tied both ends of the rope securely, then slid back down to the loft.

The rope didn't hang as low as Charlie Dick had hoped, but he wedged the board into it anyway. With a little hop, he was in himself.

"Give me a push to get me started," he instructed Miriam.

It was a marvelous swing. Charlie Dick pumped hard, going higher and higher until he was almost even with the crossbeam. His blond, sun-streaked hair flew up over his eyes each time he sailed backward, then back across his head when he swung forward, allowing him to see out of the barn, off across the green fields, over the meandering willow line that marked the creek, and to a small cluster of buildings on the farm of the closest neighbor, Jack Rupert.

Charlie Dick was so high now that at each end of his arc, the swing jerked excitingly.

Below him Miriam stood jiggling her narrow shoulders with impatience. "It's about my turn now."

Anna slid farther back near the barn wall.

The steady squeaking of the crossbeam under the moving weight was proof of Charlie Dick's unwillingness to give up the swing.

"It's my turn, Charlie Dick, and if you don't let me have it, I'm gonna tell Mama that you made a swing in the hayloft," Miriam threatened.

"She don't care," Charlie Dick replied. He knew that she would at worst only make him take it down. For a moment he did feel a little guilty about running out on Grandpa and drawing the girls away from their work. But if the girls didn't get their work done, that was their worry. Mama would scold him for not staying with Grandpa. And that would be that. "Step back, Miriam. I'm the daring young man on the flying trapeze, and I'm gonna do the death dive."

He suddenly jumped from the swing and sailed down, landing on all fours on the padded hayloft floor. The seat board of the swing flew out with him, but Miriam picked it up and quickly fitted it back into the rope. Charlie Dick sat by Anna as Miriam pumped high. She finally ended her turn with a graceless imitation of Charlie Dick's "death dive."

And so it was Anna's turn.

Charlie Dick helped her into the swing and pushed her to start, but then as Anna didn't seem to get any higher by herself, he continued pushing until she could see out the big open hatches. She smiled to herself.

Charlie Dick gave her another push. "All right, now for the death dive." He was anxious for his turn.

"Oh, I couldn't."

"Sure you can, Anna. You just wait until you start back from the highest point, then drop straight down. It's fun."

"Oh, I couldn't." Anna's dark eyes looked ahead in alarm.

"It's easy," Miriam agreed with Charlie Dick.

"I'll help you. When I say, 'now,' you jump out."

Anna didn't answer, but her hands gripped the rope tighter and her knuckles turned white.

The swing took her far up, and just as she started back, Charlie Dick shouted, "Now!"

But Anna remained in the swing, her unsmiling face fearful.

Again she reached the right point, and again Charlie Dick directed, "Now!" Once more Anna failed to respond.

"Come on, Anna. This time."

Anna's eyes were closed as the swing shot forward. Charlie Dick's mouth was open to give the command, but it remained unspoken, for suddenly Anna hurled out while the swing was still moving forward, soared out of the hayloft window like a sparrow in flight, then dropped straight down as abruptly as one shot from a BB gun.

For a moment Charlie Dick stood with his mouth open.

Miriam screamed.

Recovering from his stunned surprise, Charlie Dick ran

to the opening and peered down. Miriam crawled up beside him.

Below Anna, very still, lay in an awkward, crumpled heap.

"Oh, she's killed," Miriam shrieked.

Charlie Dick ran for the ladder. Halfway down he leaped to the middle of the horse barn floor. His bare foot brushed the bucket, tipping it over and scattering broken eggs. He dashed into the dusty yard.

"Anna!" Charlie Dick's agonized call pried at the little girl before he could reach her himself.

As Miriam came screeching from the barn, Charlie Dick bent over Anna, pulling the dark hair away from her little white face.

"She *is* killed." His older sister was by his side.

"No, she ain't, Miriam. See, she's got her eyes squinched tight shut. And quit your dumb screaming." Charlie Dick spoke with sureness, but his breath was coming in short gasps. "Anna, you're all right. Open your eyes. Anna, can you hear me? You're all right."

Gradually the tight eyelids relaxed, and Anna opened her eyes. She didn't look at them but stared straight up into space.

"Oh, Anna, I thought you were killed." Miriam stood with her hands covering her cheeks.

"She's all right, ain't you, Anna? Come on and I'll help you sit up."

Charlie Dick slid his hand under the back of her head

and carefully pushed her into a sitting position. She looked at her brother and sister a moment, then bent her dark head over her folded arms. Soft, occasional sobs could be heard from under the long hair.

"You're all right, ain't you, Anna?" Charlie Dick bit his lip worriedly.

The little head nodded, but the almost inaudible sobs kept up.

"Then why are you crying?"

When she didn't reply, both Charlie Dick and Miriam squatted down and peered under the flowing hair. Her silent tears dropped onto one arm, which was cradled painfully against her chest.

"She is too hurt. She's hurt her arm," Miriam cried, "and it's all your fault."

"My fault? It isn't any more my fault than yours."

"Yes, it is, Charlie Dick. You made her do that death dive. And you made that swing up there in the first place and coaxed us to play with you. It's your fault she's hurt, and I'm gonna tell Mama. Come on, Anna. I'll take you to the house."

Miriam put her arm around Anna's shoulder, helped her to her feet, and slowly guided her through the barnyard.

"But Anna said she wasn't hurt," Charlie Dick subdued his own doubts with words.

"Anna would never complain even if she was killed. But she's hurt her arm and maybe bad too—and all because of you, Charlie Dick."

He followed them until they reached the coalshed, and there he shooed a cat out from her sleeping place in the shade and waited anxiously, digging his bare toes into the soft dirt. Only a moment passed before he heard his mother's voice calling him from the house. He would get it now. And it wasn't really his fault Anna hurt her arm. That Miriam! He slammed his hands deep into his overall pockets and trudged around the coalshed.

Mama straightened up from leaning over Anna as Charlie Dick stepped into the doorway. Anna sat on a chair, and Charlie Dick was relieved to see that some color had returned to her face. A deep frown pulled Mama's eyebrows down almost to touch her eyelids.

"Charlie Dick, you have gone too far." She walked over to her son, took his shoulder, spun him around, and marched him back out to the coalshed. There she pushed him inside.

"You're to stay here 'til your father comes in."

She shut the door before he could object, and he heard the outside catch lock into place. Dejectedly he squatted down on a large lump of coal and rested his face in his hands. Even sitting with Grandpa wasn't as bad as being locked in the coalshed with the only thing to look forward to a whipping from Daddy. He wished Mama had punished him herself. A scolding from her, or even a whipping for that matter, wasn't nearly as bad as one stern look from his father.

Charlie Dick had piled the coal into a round fort and

smeared black dust all over himself by the time he heard the catch being pushed up. His father stepped from the sunshine into the dim shed. From his hand hung a willow stripped of its leaves.

"You've got two lickings coming, Charlie Dick."

Charlie Dick wiped his nose with the back of his hand, blackened with coal dust. "I don't care about no lickings."

"And I guess you don't care about Anna nor Grandpa either, nor your mother, who needs your cooperation." Dad pushed his hat back from his forehead. His voice was steady, but his forehead, wrinkled from opening his eyes wide to the soft light, made him look angry.

"You know I wouldn't hurt Anna. We were just having some fun."

"I guess you were just having some fun with Grandpa too. I guess you were just having some fun, and you completely forgot that I told you not to play any tricks on Grandpa. He's a sick old man. Not everything in this world is fun, Charlie Dick. And that you'll find out right now. Bend over."

The willow did smart, but it wasn't nearly as bad as Dad's lecture before, Charlie Dick thought, as he pressed his face between two lumps of coal. Not bad enough to cry about. He gritted his teeth. I can stand it longer than Daddy can.

Charlie Dick was right. After a moment John Hale threw down the willow and pulled his hat back over his forehead.

"You're to stay here in the coalshed—without your dinner. And we won't save you a piece of Grandpa's birthday cake either. You've had yours and crumbled the rest of it up pretty bad in the bargain." The big man ducked out the low doorway and locked the shed door after him.

"Doggone it, I'm hungry."

Charlie Dick leaned against the coalshed wall scratching his ankle with his toenails. He eyed a lump of coal thoughtfully. Maybe he was standing here starving with good food right under his nose. Pigs ate coal and liked it. Charlie Dick had seen them many times as they crunched it between their teeth with little pieces spilling out onto the ground. Charlie Dick himself could make a meal of coal. That would fool his family. They would expect to find him here pining away with hunger, but when they came to let him out, he would be munching happily on a big hunk of coal with his stomach sticking out contentedly. And even if he was full when they opened the door, he would take another bite just to see their faces.

He stooped down, picked up a chip of coal from the floor and plopped it in his mouth. It wasn't nearly as satisfying as he had hoped. He crushed it with his teeth, but the flavor didn't improve. Still he refused to spit it out.

At that moment he heard his name whispered. He stopped shifting the coal around in his mouth and cocked his ear up to listen.

"Charlie Dick."

He jumped toward the sound and pressed his face to a small opening in the wall.

"Anna, is that you?" Charlie Dick asked quietly as he peered out.

His little sister came into his view. One arm hung heavily in a sling made from a folded dish towel.

"I've got something for you, Charlie Dick," she whispered.

"You have, Anna? Then you're not mad at me?"

"No. And I'm sorry you got in trouble because of me," she said sadly.

"Don't you worry about that. It ain't nothing."

She looked at him worshipfully for a moment before she slipped her free hand inside her sling and drew out a large piece of cake with cherry juice-colored frosting.

"Oh, Anna!"

With force he shot the coal from his mouth out the opening into the weeds.

"Have you been eating coal?" Anna handed the cake up through the hole to him.

Charlie Dick took half the cake in one bite. "Yes, but it ain't good," he confessed with his mouth full.

She leaned against the outside of the coalshed close to him. "Mama gave me some cherry juice and Miriam helped me paint my new doll table and chair that I made yesterday. It's about dry."

Now Charlie Dick wished he had taken the time to help Anna remake her broken furniture.

"The doll doesn't have to be very big to fit them."

"O.K., Anna." But he wondered why he had ever promised Anna the doll. Anna always took him seriously even when he spoke impulsively and didn't really mean it. He only hoped Daddy wasn't too angry now to give him wages so that he could buy the doll.

He quickly changed the subject. "Your arm ain't really hurt, Anna, is it?"

She shook her head, and her long hair fell over the sling. "Just sprained a little is all."

Charlie Dick found this subject no more comfortable, so he tried again. "But how did you get that cake for me, Anna? Did you sneak it when no one was looking?"

Anna gazed admiringly at the part of her brother's coal-stained face that was visible through the opening. "I just saved you my piece."

3

Charlie Dick lifted the long lever that operated the mower blades. He pulled the reins to the right and the team obediently turned. As he drove the horses in a wide circle on the rough ground, he bounced around on the metal seat. His father had just appeared at the fence, and Charlie Dick knew he must look small on the big machine, but that made him feel even greater pride in his fine control of the animals and the mower. He felt as big as his shadow, which because of the low sun stretched halfway across the field.

He guided the horses into line with a strip of alfalfa —the only left standing—dropped the blades precisely, and clicked his tongue at the horses encouragingly. The blades moved back and forth and the green stems fell neatly behind the mower.

At the end of the strip he twisted on the seat and surveyed the whole field now flat with mown hay. It had no ragged corners like Charlie Dick sometimes saw in neighbors' fields. He grinned, his teeth showing white in his dusty face. He lifted the blades and drove over to the fence.

"All done," he called to his father as he pulled the horses to a stop and jumped off the hard seat.

"Fine job, too," John Hale complimented as he dropped the wire gate and began unhitching the team. "As fine as I've ever seen."

Although he was tired, Charlie Dick hopped about happily. Because of yesterday's incident, he had made a special effort to earn his father's praise.

Kathleen ran into view from around the barn. "Daddy, Daddy," she called.

"What is it?" Dad asked as she ran up to them.

"Daddy, Mama wants you to come to the house right now. Some men are here to see you."

"Is it Jack Rupert or some of our other neighbors?" John Hale questioned as he tugged the heavy work harnesses from the backs of the horses.

"No, it's a big tall man and one that's kind of fat, and they've got whiskers." Kathleen's blond braids bounced around as she danced excitedly before her father. "Mama wants you to come right now."

Charlie Dick closed the gate after his father had turned the horses into the pasture, and together they strode through the barnyard. Charlie Dick purposefully took long strides—almost as big as his father's—except when Kathleen, who was darting back and forth in front of him, got in the way.

"Here's Daddy," Kathleen shouted as they neared the flowing well. All the family, except Anna, were grouped around the two men, who were drinking from some tin cups. The men's clothes were dusty and ill fitting. Charlie Dick knew he had never seen them before.

Margaret Hale handed Elizabeth Eliza to Miriam and stepped to meet her husband. "They're looking for work."

Dad smiled as he reached the men. "John Hale's my name." He warmly offered his hand.

The tall stranger took his hand. "I'm Walt, and this here is Alf. And as your wife said, we're both needing work. You wouldn't be wanting a hand yourself or be able to tell us someone who does?"

"You came to the right place. I'm desperate for help, and about every farm in the valley is in the same fix." Dad shook Alf's hand. "Have you done much farm work?"

"Quite a bit," Walt said.

"For anyone around this country?" Dad asked.

"No, but I used to help my grandfather on his farm in the summer." He tugged at a button on his too-tight shirt as his gaze reached out over the farm. "We did a lot of haying there too."

"Where did you come from?" Charlie Dick asked Walt as Dad turned to speak to Alf. He wondered why his fa-

36

ther was even talking to the men about work. Charlie Dick was Dad's hired help. When Walt continued drinking from his cup, Charlie Dick insisted impolitely, "Where did you come from? Did you come through Hanging Rock?"

The tall man swirled the rest of the icy water in the tin cup before he answered. "No, we came from down country."

"The fact is I could use you both and still not get the work done around here." Dad pushed his hat back from his forehead. "But I can only afford one, and part of those wages will have to come in room and board."

Walt rubbed the dark whiskers on his chin for a moment. "It wouldn't be necessary to hire us both. We were kind of thinking of working at different places anyway. What do you say, Alf?"

"I say I'd like to be nearer town, if there is such a thing as a town in these parts." Alf leaned on a post and mopped his perspiring face with a fat hand.

"The biggest farm in the valley is just a mile from Hanging Rock. Tom Bensen owns it," Dad suggested.

"Hanging Rock is real big." Kathleen jumped up and down in front of Walt, "but it's not as big as White River. White River has got two show houses."

Walt smiled at Kathleen and patted her bobbing head. "You go ahead to the Bensen place, Alf, and if you get a chance, have yourself a good time in Hanging Rock." He turned to Dad. "And if you'll have me, Mr. Hale, I'll stay right here."

"We'd be pleased to have you." Dad again offered his hand.

"Goody," said Kathleen.

Miriam swung Elizabeth Eliza in a circle.

Mama's face was lit up the same as when she saw the first buttercup of spring. "You're an answer to a prayer."

"But *I'm* working for you." Charlie Dick couldn't believe his father had really hired someone else. It wasn't as though Charlie Dick was a poor worker. "I mowed that whole field behind the barn today."

"Yes, and a fine job he did too," Dad spoke to everyone, then added to his son, "and we'll still need your help. There's plenty of work around here, you know that. And the days I haven't got a special job for you, you can help your mother. She probably needs help worse than I do."

"In the house?" Charlie Dick asked in disbelief.

Miriam snickered in her hand, but no one else was interested in how he felt.

"If you can help Charlie Dick with the chores, Walt, I'll drop Alf by the Bensen farm," Dad offered. "It's a long walk, and one of us would need to go to town tomorrow for medicine for Grandpa anyway."

"Fine," agreed Walt.

Charlie Dick watched the whole group walk across the yard to the pickup. That snicker of Miriam's had crystallized his feelings. He felt indignation growing inside him toward all his family, who always treated him just as though he were only another daughter. But he felt a spe-

38

cial resentment toward the big man who would do his work while he did a girl's job. And after he had worked so hard today. The muscles in his arm still ached from pulling the heavy mower lever. Charlie Dick kicked a clod with his bare foot before he slowly followed after the others to the pickup.

Dad was peering through the window at his set of keys dangling from the ignition, where he always left them.

"Oh, dear," Mama said, "Anna and Kathleen were playing in the truck this afternoon. They must have locked it somehow with your keys inside." She took Elizabeth Eliza from Miriam. "Run in the house and get my set from the medicine shelf in the kitchen."

Miriam trotted off on her thin legs. The men chatted about the weather. It seemed a long time before Miriam came back outside. She was pulling Anna by the hand that wasn't in the sling.

"I couldn't find your keys, Mama. They weren't on the medicine shelf, and I looked everywhere in the kitchen."

"Where in the world can they be?" puzzled Mama.

"I think Elizabeth Eliza had them this morning," offered Kathleen.

"For heaven's sake, Kathleen, when you see Elizabeth Eliza with them take them away from her," Margaret Hale corrected, a little embarrassed that this confusing predicament should happen in front of strangers.

"Anna and Kathleen should have to look for them." Miriam gave her opinion. "They locked Daddy's keys in the pickup, so it's all their fault. And Anna's the oldest."

Anna kept her eyes timidly on the ground, afraid to look at the two men. "We didn't mean to lock it," she worried.

Charlie Dick felt much more sorry for Anna than for Kathleen, who screwed up her face and started to howl. "I don't think you need to blame Anna." He threw himself into the fray.

"There is no use blaming anyone." John Hale took hold of the situation. "We'll just all have to go in and look until we find Mother's keys. Let's get right at it and hope we can find them soon. Alf doesn't want to stand here waiting all night."

"Maybe I can help you," Walt proposed.

"You needn't look for them," Mama replied.

"I mean maybe I could fiddle with the lock and get it open for you."

"Do you think you could?" Mama asked hopefully.

"Maybe," Walt said, "but I'll need a piece of thin wire."

"I'll bet I could get it open with the can opener on Grandpa's big pocketknife," Charlie Dick said as Dad fished a piece of chicken wire from his pocket, but no one paid any attention to him.

Walt put his ear down near the door handle and listened to the wire as it clicked inside the keyhole. The Hale family crowded around him and watched silently as he flicked the wire first one way, then another.

"Yes, I think I can get it," he said after a moment. Then following a hard twist, he tugged at the handle.

Down it snapped and then the door swung wide open.

Miriam's surprised gasp turned to a coo of admiration.

"Thank you, Walt." John Hale climbed in and unlocked the other door for Alf.

"I really don't know how we would have managed that without you," Mama complimented the new hired hand as the pickup drove out of the yard into the lane.

Charlie Dick had started milking Buttons without offering to show Walt how he could help. However, Walt found a stool, some hobbles, and a pail and began milking.

The tinny sound of the milk hitting the bottom of the hired man's bucket contrasted with the full, frothy sound in Charlie Dick's.

Walt chuckled. "It's been a long time since I milked."

Charlie Dick didn't answer, but his hands worked faster to increase the difference between them. Dad had sure pulled a boner, he thought, hiring a worker so slow that he couldn't even match a ten-year-old boy.

Charlie Dick finished Buttons and turned her out of the barn. "When you're through," Charlie Dick said to Walt, "pour your milk into the bucket with mine and bring it to the house." He left the barn and walked through the moonless night around the corrals. He would go to the house, he told himself, sit around, and wait for Walt. Then his family would know how slow Walt was.

As he rounded the chicken coop, he suddenly stopped, for he heard movement ahead of him at the woodpile.

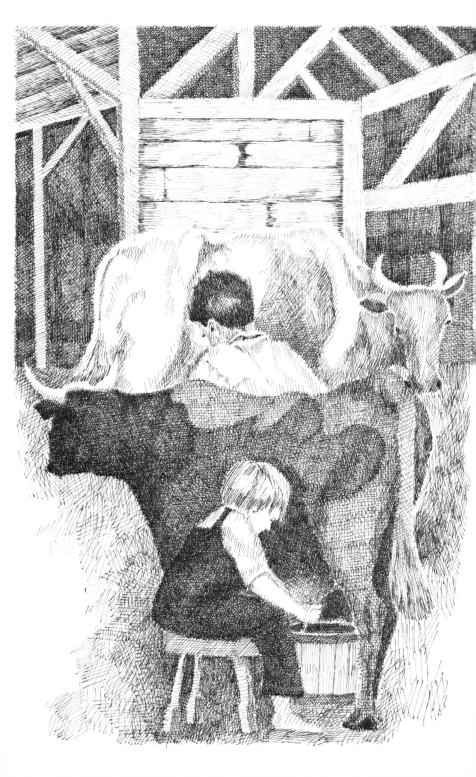

Feeling with his bare toes for silent places to step, he crept through the darkness guided by the thud of wood being stacked.

"The next time you don't gather enough when it's your turn to bring in the wood, I'll . . . I'll . . . ," Miriam's voice threatened quietly, "I can't see a thing I'm doing."

"I brought in two armloads this morning," whimpered Kathleen.

Charlie Dick crouched motionless behind an uncut pile of kindling wood.

"Yes, with about one stick each time," Miriam scolded in her subdued voice, "and now I have to come out and help you 'cause you're such a scaredy cat."

Kathleen began her crybaby howl.

"Do you think I like it out here in the dark any more than you do? And keep your voice down."

Kathleen's loud cry stopped suddenly. "Why?" she whispered. "What would hear me?"

"I don't know. Nothing, I guess. Let's go back to the house. What wood I've got will do for tonight."

Charlie Dick stretched his head above the kindling wood and not loudly but with beautiful artistry, breathed out a wicked witch laugh. "He he he he."

The woodpile seemed to explode with Miriam's shriek; wood thrown from the girls' arms crashed about, one stick landing very near Charlie Dick. The long drawn-out scream moved with surprising speed toward the lighted doorway of the house. Miriam ran into the bright circle with Kathleen only a step behind.

"A witch! It was a witch!" Kathleen cried.

Mama, with Elizabeth Eliza on one hip, flung open the screen. "What in the world is the matter?"

Miriam's words tumbled over each other. "There's a witch out there. We heard it laugh. It was real close." Kathleen had worked up her cry into a loud howl. "It chased us on its broomstick."

Charlie Dick, unseen in the darkness, stood up and, mischievously laughing to himself, sauntered toward the house. Gee, that had been fun!

"It was just Charlie Dick," Mama assumed.

"Charlie Dick?"

"Yes, Charlie Dick. You should know it would be Charlie Dick. Now bring me that wood so I can warm up some supper."

"I'm not going back out there." Miriam pushed into the doorway with Mama. "Not for nothing. Charlie Dick can bring in the wood for being so mean. I'm sure not going to."

"Me, too," Kathleen whimpered.

Charlie Dick stepped into the light. "He he he he," he repeated his earlier performance, then laughed loudly.

"Charlie Dick, you're awful," sniffed Miriam.

"You'll have to go back and bring some wood, Charlie Dick," Mama ordered.

"But Mama," Charlie Dick argued, "I've done my work today. I did all that mowing and then I did the chores. The wood is the girls' job." Then since Kathleen was already crying, he pulled his special face at her.

"Now he's smiling at me," Kathleen bawled louder.

"Charlie Dick, I have to have some wood . . .," Mama began.

At that moment Walt walked into the yard carrying a bucket of milk. Kindling was stacked under his free arm.

"I heard you all talking about needing wood, Mrs. Hale, so I brought some while I was coming."

Everyone forgot Charlie Dick.

"Oh, Walt," Mama was pleased, "that was so thoughtful."

Miriam held open the screen so Walt could take his load inside. Kathleen trotted at his heels, and the door banged shut behind them all. Charlie Dick stood outside all alone.

Feeling very cross, Charlie Dick had been sitting by himself on the back step for some time when the pickup drove into the yard. After a moment Dad came along the board sidewalk. He stopped when he saw his son.

"Oh, Charlie Dick," he said, "I've got something I want to show you."

"O.K." This special attention from his father made Charlie Dick quite happy again.

Dad sat down by him and pulled a bottle from the sack he was carrying. "See this medicine for Grandpa. Do you know how much it cost?"

"No," Charlie Dick answered, "but I guess it cost a lot."

"You're right. But Grandpa has got to have it." He placed it back in the sack. "And the money we'll need for it and to pay Walt's hire is more cash than we've got—at least for now."

Charlie Dick's uneasiness returned with the mention of Walt.

"So that means I won't be able to pay you wages like we talked about. I hope you're not too disappointed."

"No," Charlie Dick lied, "it don't make no difference."

John Hale patted his son on the back as he stood up, but he didn't go in the house for a moment. "I'm sorry about it. Maybe later in the summer things will work out better, especially if the crickets don't move in. Tonight Tom Bensen said he'd heard they were bad down south already, but I haven't seen many here." Dad opened the door. "Come on in. I imagine your mother has some supper ready."

"O.K.," Charlie Dick answered. But he sat there for a while longer trying to absorb his disappointment before he went inside to join his family.

The night air was sweet with the smell of new-mown hay. Charlie Dick lay on his cot in the porch wearing his underwear. All he could see of Walt was the red tip of his cigarette. At supper John Hale had politely asked Walt that he not smoke in the house since the family were opposed to smoking and especially since Grandpa was very sick. Walt evidently didn't consider the porch, which

Charlie Dick was going to have to share with him, as part of the house. Nor did it occur to him to ask Charlie Dick, whose private quarters he had invaded, if he minded his smoking there.

"It's quiet out here," Walt said in a relaxed tone.

Charlie Dick tucked his hands under his head without answering.

"Nice and quiet."

"It ain't always quiet like this with only the crickets singing," Charlie Dick broke his silence. "Sometimes in the middle of the night the coyotes howl. They come down from the hills to hunt rabbits, and sometimes a rabbit squeals. You ain't never heard nothing scary until you heard the dying squeal of a rabbit."

Walt laughed pleasantly. "I don't scare too easy."

That Walt had laughed aside his comment made Charlie Dick's irritation grow. "The worst noise, though, is the mice. They run through the walls and scratch loud. They'll start moving pretty soon. They'll keep you awake, for sure." Charlie Dick couldn't keep the hopefulness from his voice.

"They won't bother me," was Walt's reply, "not a bit. And there's nothing like good hard farm work to give you a sense of well-being and make you sleep well. I was slow tonight with the chores, but I'll get onto everything again soon. I like it here. It's a good place to work—a good place to be." He paused, then asked in a friendly tone, "What are your favorite things to do around here?"

"Havn't got none," replied Charlie Dick sullenly.

"You must have something you like to do—fish or something."

"Nope," he said shortly.

Walt stood up. "Oh, well, I guess I'll walk down to the barn and listen to the frogs sing from over on the creek. If you want to come, you can."

Charlie Dick didn't reply. He thought he saw the big man shrug before he walked out of the porch and away through the yard.

Charlie Dick lay there a long time thinking over the annoying events of the day. Maybe, he finally decided, maybe if Walt didn't find the Hale place so much to his liking, he would'nt stay around long. Then things for Charlie Dick would be just like they had been before he came. He was listening to the scurrying of the mice in the old walls, wondering how to get Walt to leave when he heard his footsteps coming back through the yard. On impulse he sprang from the cot and pressed his body against the board wall. He hardly breathed as Walt pulled open the creaky door and stepped inside the dark porch. The big man paused there with his back to Charlie Dick.

"Stick 'em up." Charlie Dick made his voice low and harsh.

In the darkness he saw the man's silhouette spin around. He ducked downward as a huge fist pounded into the board where his head had been. He tried to crawl around the legs, but the big hands found him and roughly pulled him up.

"What are you trying to do?" the hired man demanded angrily.

"Can't you take a joke?" Charlie Dick flung out the words.

Suddenly he found himself spinning through the air. He landed on his cot, banging his head into the wall.

Walt, standing over him in the dimness, appeared to tower to the ceiling. "I could have killed you if I'd hit you instead of the wall. Don't you ever try another cockeyed stunt like that."

Charlie Dick lay very still. Only his rapid breathing gave away his alarm. He could hear Walt's breath coming fast too as the big man pulled off his shirt. Although he felt pleased to have upset him so easily, Charlie Dick was startled at his quick retaliation. Only his father had ever punished him physically before. He closed his eyes and groaned inwardly over the painful throbbing of his head.

If Walt wanted to be enemies that was all right with Charlie Dick. That was just fine. Charlie Dick hadn't wanted him here in the first place. And since Walt couldn't take a joke, it would be easy to pull tricks on him and make him mad.

Charlie Dick opened his eyes for a moment and looked at the stars, then closed them to still the pain in his head. Now he knew just how to make Walt find the Hale place less to his liking. Charlie Dick would pester him every minute of every day. It would be easy and kind of entertaining too, like throwing stones at magpies.

4

Charlie Dick sat on the hard wooden chair in Grandpa's room. He tapped his foot nervously on the floor, wondering if he would explode with impatience in the long hour that stretched ahead of him. Yesterday the mowing had been finished, and Charlie Dick wouldn't be able to start raking until the alfalfa stocks were partly dry. Today Dad had said that he and Walt could handle the ditching and irrigating, so for Charlie Dick to help Mama by sitting with Grandpa again, this time without running off. To make matters worse, today Grandpa was grumpier than ever.

"You say he ain't from Wyoming?" the old man abruptly demanded.

"Nope. I think he's from some big city, but he don't say much."

"Humph," Grandpa snorted, "you can't get a hired man that's worth his salt anyway, and this one a city feller." The old eyes darted about, glaring at the bedroom as though it were a prison. "Why, I used to be the fastest stacker in the whole country. There wasn't a hay crew anywhere that could keep up with me."

In the long, weary silence that followed, Charlie Dick slapped his hands alternately together, then on his knees in rhythm to Pease Porridge Hot. "The girls and Mama think he's just wonderful and Dad says he's a good worker, but I don't think he's so hot."

"A good worker! Humph! I might be old and decrepit but I still got enough sense to know that no city feller knows which end of a cow to milk." He lay with his white eyebrows drawn angrily together.

Charlie Dick warmed up, pleased that Grandpa felt the same way he did. "You should have seen him milk the first night he came." He didn't add that Walt was now nearly as fast as anyone. "I can milk a lot better than him. Daddy's got him out irrigating today, but I'll bet I could do every bit as good a job if I only got the chance."

"And no city feller knows how to make a dam that can keep from washing out for more than thirty minutes."

"You know what I did last night, Grandpa?" Charlie Dick's enthusiasm was growing. "After he went to sleep, I put eggs in his shoes. He woke up this morning and shoved a foot down in his shoe. Crack! When he pulled it out, egg yolk was dripping from between his toes." Then a new idea occurred to him. He jumped up and leaned over Grandpa and said slyly, "No, that Walt is just a city feller like you say, Grandpa. You ought to get Daddy to get rid of him."

But Grandpa pounced on him as quickly as one of the barn cats on a granary mouse. "Don't get me in on any of your schemes, Charlie Dick. I'll tell your Dad what I think, not what you want me to."

Charlie Dick sat back down. He joggled restlessly for several minutes before he reached in his pocket and pulled out a length of string. After untangling it, he threw one end out from him as though he were casting a fishing line.

"I caught a trout over at the creek last week." He threw his string out once more before he fibbed, "It was a big one."

Grandpa didn't look at him as he jumped up and began pulling in his line pretending he had a ten-pound fighter on the other end.

"Bigger than Walt could catch."

Suddenly Grandpa's old voice snapped. "Why don't you go outside to do your fishing? There's no use you staying in here and both of us being mad at each other."

"Grandpa, can I?" Charlie Dick cried, not caring in the least that it was Grandpa's annoyance at his squirming that was bringing him release from the hated duty, which always seemed to last longer than a cow's cud.

"Yes, go on. There's no need at all for you being here."

"Thanks, Grandpa. You know what I'll do? I'll go fishing over at the creek, that's what I'll do. I'll fish and fish and fish until I catch a real big one. Mama can cook it, and it'll be just for you alone, Grandpa. For your dinner." He gave a couple of leaps in the air. "Thanks, Grandpa."

Charlie Dick went to the creek, but he didn't go fishing. Instead he played war with Miriam and Anna. When they had chased each other to the far end of the pasture, Charlie Dick decided to have a swim at the beaver dam.

"Why do you want to go swimming, Charlie Dick?" Miriam asked as they came through the willows to the edge of the pond. "Let's finish our war." She carried a tall ragweed, stripping the leaves from it to make it into a spear in case their game did continue.

"We're through with war. I already won that game." Charlie Dick swished the water with his hand to test its temperature.

"You did not win, Charlie Dick. I hit you four times with my spears, and you only hit me twice," Miriam argued.

"Now, Miriam, you know I won." When Anna came struggling through the weeds into view, he appealed to her with a grin. "Didn't I, Anna?"

The little girl nodded solemnly.

Charlie Dick began to unbutton his shirt.

"Charlie Dick, you know Mama doesn't want you swimming in the beaver pond. And I'll tell her if you do. Come on. Let's finish our game."

"She don't care." Even though he knew she did, he unsnapped the buckle on his bib overalls.

"And what are you going to wear swimming? You can't go swimming without a gunnysack or something."

Charlie Dick pulled off his shirt. "I'm going to wear my birthday suit, that's what."

"You're awful," Miriam whined. "And I'll tell Mama. Come on, Anna, let's go."

She grabbed Anna's hand, the one free from the sling, and with her narrow shoulders raised in indignation dragged her little sister through the willows in a hurry to get out of sight before her brother was completely undressed. Anna smiled back at Charlie Dick.

When the girls were outside the wall of trees, Miriam called back, "Charles Richard Hale, you're awful, and I did too win at war—four to two."

"No, you didn't," Charlie Dick joked as he slid into the pond his feet sinking into the thick mud on the bottom.

"Liar, liar, your pants are on fire. I hit you four times when we were down at the other end of the pasture by Buttons and the other cows."

Charlie Dick put off going after the fish for Grandpa until late afternoon. He decided he would walk over to the pasture after the cows a little early so he would have a few minutes to throw a line in the water, but he was just leaving the house when Mama found a job for him.

"Charlie Dick," Mama said, "take this snack over to Walt. He's irrigating in the east field, and your dad said he'll be working there until after dark, and he won't get supper until late."

"Oh,, Mama, do I have to?" Charlie Dick screwed up his face.

"Yes, you . . ."

"I'll do it," Charlie Dick suddenly interrupted. Then

afraid that his sudden enthusiasm would arouse suspicion, he added casually, "I mean it will be a long jaunt to the east field, but I don't mind doing it. Can I make a sandwich to eat on the way?"

"Yes, but don't dawdle too long." She left the kitchen to attend to Elizabeth Eliza, who was crying upstairs.

Charlie Dick wasted no time in making a new sandwich—two slices of unbuttered bread with a cracker in the center. He paused before wrapping it in place of the crabapple jelly sandwich Mama had made.

"Just in case that's not dry enough . . ." He reached for the chili powder and sprinkled it generously on the cracker. Then he quickly substituted some warm water from the tea-kettle for the cold well water in the canteen and, just for good measure, he added a generous amount of vinegar.

With his shadow stretching long in front of him, he walked rapidly through the yards toward the east field. He took large mouthfuls of the jelly sandwich and chewed it hastily, his cheeks bulging. He chuckled as he licked some jelly from his fingers.

"Ummmmm, Walt's sandwich was sure good," he said aloud. He patted the sack that contained the canteen and other sandwich and broke into a run.

Charlie Dick could see Walt standing in Dad's hip boots in the middle of the irrigation ditch shoveling mud onto the canvas dam. The hired man looked up when he approached but continued working until the water backed

up, overflowing the main channel into the shallow side ditch and onto the field of green wheat.

"Mama sent this sack for you." Charlie Dick handed it to him when he stepped onto the bank.

Walt opened the bag and pulled out the canteen. "That water will taste good. It's been mighty hot here this afternoon." He unwrapped the sandwich.

Charlie Dick stepped back a few paces. Walt noticed him watching intently. He paused with the bread at his lips.

"And thanks for bringing it over."

"You're welcome." Charlie Dick was all meekness.

Walt took a big bite. He looked a little startled at first taste, but chewed a couple of times before the chili powder dissolved. Suddenly he spit the mouthful into the ditch and twisted at the lid of the canteen with a howl.

"Maybe Miriam made that sandwich," Charlie Dick suggested innocently as Walt frantically shoved the container to his lips. "Sometimes she sure cooks up some awful stuff."

The vinegar water shot from Walt's mouth with a gurgling roar.

"Once she made a cake without any sugar. The pigs wouldn't even eat it."

Walt's eyes narrowed. "Miriam nothing. That's the last of your tricks for today, Charlie Dick." His hand shot out for the boy's shoulder, but Charlie Dick spun out of reach and tried to dash off. Even though the big boots held him back, Walt was right with him, clutching his arm. Charlie

Dick ducked down as Walt brought the canteen near his face.

"I hear vinegar is good for the hair." Walt poured the whole contents of the canteen over Charlie Dick's head before he let him go.

Charlie Dick stumbled out of reach. "I sure hope that chili powder don't give you a bellyache," he called to the big man, refusing to admit that he had been bested. His eyes smarted from the vinegar water all the long way back to the house.

Charlie Dick carried the bowl of chicken broth from the kitchen. He passed Anna sitting on the living room floor with her doll furniture and went into Grandpa's bedroom. Mama had assigned her son the job of feeding Grandpa his supper because Charlie Dick had not stayed his full time with the old man in the morning. Charlie Dick sat down on the chair by the bed. Just as he had many hours before, old Charles Hale lay with his eyebrows drawn into a frown.

"I brought you your supper." Charlie Dick held the bowl down so he could look into it.

"I see it ain't the fish you said you'd catch."

"No, I guess not," Charlie Dick had to admit, "but I'll be sure to catch one for you tomorrow," he promised carelessly.

"Oh, don't bother. I don't want a fish anyway," Grandpa scolded sourly, "but you ought not to make promises you're not going to keep, and you ought to keep the promises you make. It ain't right, that's all. You keep your promises after this."

Charlie Dick did feel a little guilty about not getting Grandpa's fish, but when he glanced through the doorway at Anna in the living room with her doll furniture, his conscience felt as prickly as a gunnysack bathing suit. But how could he get Anna her doll without the wages which Walt had taken from him, Charlie Dick excused himself quickly.

Charlie Dick spooned some broth into Grandpa's mouth, but the old man was little interested in the food.

"What has Walt been doing this afternoon?" he demanded.

"He's been over in the east field watering," Charlie Dick answered. Several drops of broth splashed out onto the sheet. "But I took him over a chili sandwich and some vinegar water. Wow, did he ever spit it out fast." He didn't mention why his own eyes were red.

"You think that's funny, don't you?"

Charlie Dick was surprised at Grandpa's displeasure, especially since he didn't like Walt being at the Hales' either.

"No, I ain't mean," Charlie Dick protested, wiping at the drops he had spilled on the sheet. "With nothing important to do and just girls around and nobody fun to play with, I just make some fun to liven things up. If I could have been young when you were a little boy and gone hunting bears up on Bald Mountain and stuff like you did with your brothers . . . But a feller can't do nothing exciting now," he finished.

Grandpa grumbled. "Ain't that like kids, wishing their lives away. Did you ever stop to think that if you'd been young then, you'd be old now—just lying in bed and having others wait on you?"

"It would be worth it."

"Humph," Grandpa snorted.

"It would. I wouldn't lie there being grumpy like you are. No sir. Instead of being cross I'd just remember all the exciting times I'd had, like when the Indians came and I was the only one home, and I wasn't a bit afraid and wouldn't let them take our good cow. Yes, it'd be worth it." Charlie Dick lifted another spoonful of broth. "Yes, I'd lie in bed and think about all the wonderful things I'd done."

Charles Hale didn't open his mouth to the food. His old face looked startled.

"Don't you want the rest of this?" Charlie Dick waggled the spoon a little, hoping Grandpa would soon be finished so he could leave.

"Huh?" Grandpa asked, but he stared at the ceiling as though Charlie Dick weren't there at all.

"Don't you want the rest of this?" Charlie Dick repeated louder.

Finally Grandpa glanced at the spoon. "Oh, no more." He looked vacant, as though he had just lost something valuable.

And Charlie Dick wondered what he was brooding about now to make him so unhappily thoughtful.

5

Anna had walked over to meet Charlie Dick at noon. He was glad to see that her arm was now free from the sling, but he didn't comment on it. She trotted along beside Charlie Dick as he strode up the lane. Dad was back at the stackyard and Walt was almost to the barns.

"What's for dinner?" Charlie Dick asked. "I'm hungry as a bear."

"Strawberries," Anna mentioned the item that seemed most important to her. "Mama skimmed enough cream off last night's milk for them, and I picked the strawberries. Miriam was supposed to, but she couldn't because she was looking for her brooch."

"Her brooch?" Charlie Dick asked quickly.

"Yes, the pretty pin that was Grandma Hale's before she died. Miriam looked and looked all morning. Then she cried and said she knew someone had stolen it because she always kept it in the little box on her shelf. Mama said no one around here would steal it." While she related the morning's happenings, Anna's tone had become very sober, and now she worried to Charlie Dick. "Do you think someone stole it, Charlie Dick?"

"Oh, no, Anna," Charlie Dick reassured her. "You don't need to worry a bit about that." When Anna's face still looked troubled, he continued, "In fact, I know right where it is, but don't you tell anybody."

"I won't," Anna agreed quickly, but then she asked, "Will Miriam get it back soon?"

"Sure, Anna. Real soon, but don't tell."

Dad, driving the team, came up beside them, and Anna's glance told Charlie Dick her lips were sealed.

"Do you want to ride the rest of the way?" John Hale stopped the horses and lifted Anna up.

Charlie Dick patted his pocket with the heavy brooch inside as he ran ahead to catch up with Walt. He smiled smugly as he walked behind him toward the flowing well. Walt kept absent-mindedly reaching in his pocket or nervously rubbing his lips. It was plain to Charlie Dick that Walt was miserable. After the failure with the chili sandwich Charlie Dick had decided that more subtle tricks might be safer, and now he was finding them more effective too.

Actually it had been simple to hide Walt's cigarettes last night when the big man was getting ready for bed. Walt tossed the packs from his pockets onto his cot and then turned his back for a moment to look out into the night. With one deft movement Charlie Dick had scooped them up and shoved them in a bushel basket of empty fruit jars stored in the porch. Sleight of hand, Charlie Dick complimented himself.

Now at the flowing well, Charlie Dick again got the chance to see how quickly he could work. Walt took off his shirt, shook the dust and hay leaves from it and tossed it onto a fence post. He bent over the water to wash. Quickly Charlie Dick pinned Miriam's brooch on his shirt, then leaned against the fence, pretending unconcern. The big man pulled his shirt back on, but his trembling fingers fumbled with the buttons. Distracted without his cigarettes, he did not see the gleaming jewelry on his chest. Wow, would he be mad when he noticed what a sissy he looked like! Sleight of hand, Charlie Dick noted again. I'm so good I'll be a magician when I grow up. That's just what I'll be.

In the house Charlie Dick walked to the stove through the confusion of the last minute dinner preparations. Walt stopped inside the kitchen door.

"Did you have a good morning, Walt?" Mama greeted the hired man.

"We got a lot of hay stacked. But you haven't seen my cigarettes around, have you? I'm missing them."

"For heaven's sake, everything is missing," Mama said without looking up from the gravy she was stirring. "Miriam's keepsake brooch is gone too. We're way behind in

our work because we've wasted half the morning looking for it."

Miriam, who sniffled and dabbed at her red eyes, was setting the table.

Charlie Dick scooped some mashed potatoes from the pan on the back of the stove and pretended not to notice Elizabeth Eliza, who toddled over to Walt with her chubby finger pointing at the decorated front.

"Petty, petty," the baby said.

Despite her swollen eyes, Miriam giggled as she carried a stack of plates to the table. "Elizabeth Eliza said you're pretty, Walt."

"Petty, petty," the toddler continued.

"Elizabeth Eliza, Walt's not pretty." Kathleen walked over to correct her baby sister. "He's . . ." she paused.

"Handsome," Mama said quickly before Kathleen could say some other word.

"Your brooch, Miriam." Kathleen stared at Walt's bright front. "Your brooch!"

Then all the family saw.

"My brooch," shrieked Miriam.

For the first time Walt looked down at his shirt. "Why, I . . ." he began in confusion. "How did . . . What . . . ?"

"Petty," cooed Elizabeth Eliza again.

Everybody stared at Walt.

"But I didn't . . ." Walt hemmed and hawed. "I wouldn't . . ."

"Charlie Dick, have you been up to one of your tricks?" Mama asked. "Why, we've wasted all morning looking for that," she scolded. She turned to soothe Walt, who was still obviously distressed. "Don't you worry about it, Walt. It was just Charlie Dick. You know how Charlie Dick is."

"Charlie Dick? Oh, sure, it would be Charlie Dick."

"Charlie Dick, what have you been doing? Taking my brooch that was Grandma Hale's? Mama, make Charlie Dick stay out of my things," yelled Miriam.

Charlie Dick bulged his eyes at her.

When Walt unpinned the brooch and handed it to her, she told him, "That Charlie Dick! We know you wouldn't take it, Walt."

"Thanks," Walt replied gratefully.

Kathleen took his hand. Walt smiled down at her.

Barking like a dog, Charlie Dick zipped past everyone, ducked out the door, and headed for the flowing well to wash. Oh, Walt had been mighty embarrassed, Charlie Dick reflected as he dipped his fingers into the cold water. Just to be on the safe side, he would stay out of Walt's way for a while. But it didn't seem too bright of him not to realize right away that Charlie Dick was the one who had pinned the jewelry on his shirt.

"I'm afraid we're going to have a fight on our hands before summer is over," Dad said at the dinner table.

"Are they that bad?" Mama asked. With the arm that

wasn't holding Elizabeth Eliza, she passed the gravy to Walt.

"We haven't got anything compared to what the farms farther south have got. The crickets move with the wind. They've just begun to hit down valley, but they're bad there already."

"They sure was thick this morning at the haystack where I was riding derrick horse," Charlie Dick interjected into his parents' conversation. Then he watched Kathleen as he continued, "But if we have to, we can eat them. Indians used to eat grasshoppers. First, they would roast 'em, and when they was all crispy, they would pluck off a leg, crunch, crunch . . ."

"Charlie Dick!" Kathleen wailed.

"Charlie Dick, you mean thing." Miriam, still irritated about her brooch, continued, "Daddy, do you know what Charlie Dick did?" and she told him in detail the happenings of the morning.

Dad frowned at Charlie Dick but made no comment. When Charlie Dick winked at Anna, she winked back.

All during dinner the girls and Mama were especially attentive to Walt to make up for his earlier discomfort. Happy with the attention, he was more talkative than usual.

"My grandmother used to make gravy just like this, Mrs. Hale," he said. "It sure is good."

"There's nothing like hard work to make a man appreciate food." Mama gave a little laugh of pleasure as she brushed the compliment aside.

"In fact you cook a lot like my grandmother did when I'd stay at the farm when I was a kid. A good cook she was. And a good woman. And she was pretty too. She had dark eyes like Anna's, and her skin was light too. Yes, she was pretty like you, Anna."

The soft pink that appeared in Anna's cheeks told of her delight.

"In the city I didn't have nothing to do, but I worked hard on the farm in the summers. Grandpa made me work hard, but he was good to me. I guess being on the farm was the only decent time I ever had."

As Walt continued, telling about the calf his grandpa said could be his and the shirt his grandmother sewed for him, all the girls listened raptly. Charlie Dick expected Miriam and Kathleen to be admiring, but for Anna to be equally interested was very distressing. So when Walt, just for Anna, described a big doll with a china head his grandmother always had sitting on a cushion on one end of her sofa, Charlie Dick just couldn't stand it any more.

He left the table, picked the paring knife off the cupboard and stuffed it quickly into the big pocket of his overalls. When he caught Anna's eyes, he motioned for her to come with him. At the door he whispered in her ear. "Come over to the haystack this afternoon. I want to show you something."

Anna nodded.

Charlie Dick quickly left the house and started for the creek. He found a dry branch near the water, cut it from the dead willow and sat down in the shade. He scratched rapidly at the wood with the paring knife until a shape began to form.

"It's easy to tell," Charlie Dick said to himself as he squinted at the stick he held at arm's length. "Yes, it's easy to tell *that* is a head." He picked up some straw from the ground and folded it over the rounded portion of the stick. "A head with golden hair."

It was late afternoon, and Charlie Dick had long ago finished the willow doll and dropped it into his pocket when Anna came trudging through the field with grasshoppers spilling away in front of her.

"I've got something for you," Charlie Dick smiled pleasantly at his little sister as she reached him.

In Anna's silence her delicate skin glowed pink.

"I've got something for you that I've been promising for a long time."

She dug her toes into the dirt—so full of hope that her eyes couldn't meet Charlie Dick's.

"Do you want to see it?"

She nodded her head with a quick little jerk.

Slowly Charlie Dick drew from his pocket the awkwardly carved wooden figure. The straw slipped from its head, but he quickly patted it back into place.

"I've got a doll for you like I promised." He held it out to Anna. "Here, take it."

She looked up for the first time, her eyes as bright as thimbles. Slowly the eagerness died from her face, and it became impenetrable. But she took the misshapen figure from her brother's hand and turned it slowly around.

"Thanks," her tiny voice said mechanically. Her shoulders sagged.

For a moment Charlie Dick felt some of the misery that it seemed Anna's lot always to carry. No, it would not do. Not at all.

"It's only until I get the real one for you—with long blond hair."

The disappointment flowed out of Anna like irrigation water from a ditch with the headgate lifted.

She tucked the carved stick inside the pocket of her dress, a too long hand-me-down from Miriam, before she turned and walked back through the field to the house.

No, it wouldn't do at all. Somehow Charlie Dick really would have to keep his promise about the doll. Because of Anna's disappointment, he fully realized that it wasn't right not to keep it, as Grandpa had said. But how could Charlie Dick ever get a doll like Anna wanted? There was no way as long as Walt was at the farm doing work Charlie Dick could do just as well and earning Charlie Dick's wages. And Walt had turned out to be as tenacious as a cow newly separated from her calf hanging around the calf pen. Charlie Dick had just been too easy on Walt. This very afternoon he would think up something drastic.

Charlie Dick stood at the fence inside the stackyard and watched the huge black and white bull eat from the pile of hay he had thrown over the fence to him. The animal's large head tossed the remaining hay up over his powerful shoulders. His thick neck lifted his head high as he walked back to the middle of his pen.

Charlie Dick bent down and scooted under the wires of the fence. The bull turned to face him, and his nostrils grew large. Charlie Dick danced about provokingly.

The bull lowered his head and pawed the earth. Dust rose around him. In imitation Charlie Dick dropped to his knees and scooped dirt with his hands, sending it flying behind him. Snorting, the bull ran at the boy.

It was a simple matter for Charlie Dick to roll under the fence to safety before he came near. As the big Holstein swung away from the fence, Charlie Dick gathered a handful of pebbles and peppered the dark hide. The powerful animal nervously paced about his pen and trumpeted his raucous cry of rage.

A plan began to form in Charlie Dick's mind. "I wonder," he asked the bull, "if you've ever met our hired hand, Walt."

Walt had driven his team and rack from the yard after unloading his hay when Charlie Dick called to him, "You left your pitchfork on the stack." Charlie Dick himself had tossed it back there while Walt was climbing down.

"Bring it to me," the big man called.

"Get it yourself," Charlie Dick countered.

Walt's eyes narrowed. Immediately Charlie Dick was on guard ready to run if the big man should come after him. But Walt only shrugged, looped the reins around the center post of the rack and jumped down.

Charlie Dick ducked behind the stack and slipped the loop off the gate post. The wire gate fell to the ground. Walt had just leaped from the stack and was standing in front of the fork he had dropped down before him as Charlie Dick bounded past him. The hired man's large hands reached out and caught the back straps of his bib overalls. But Charlie Dick jerked from his grasp and flung himself against the stack just as the bull plowed into view. Startled, Walt stood unprotected in the center of the yard.

The bull plunged forward, his feet stirring up a cloud of dry hay leaves. As the huge head came near, the hired man grabbed up his fork and swung it. The flat of the tines knocked the neck to one side. The bull twirled to face him, but Walt fled to the closest fence and dived through the wires. Charlie Dick heard his clothes rip on the barbs.

The wires of the fence creaked under the weight of the animal's body against it. But they held. The bull faced back to the yard.

Then Charlie Dick realized his exposed position. The stack rose steeply above him—too steeply to make it rapidly to safety. With head lowered, the bull pawed the dirt. Charlie Dick sidled slowly along the edge of the stack, hoping his cautious movement would not attract the bull. But with an angry bellow the huge animal sprang toward him.

Charlie Dick bolted toward the nearest safety—the tall wooden derrick. The earth shook behind him. He leaped for the wooden support. As he scrambled up the sloping beam, he felt the bull's hot breath on his bare foot. The wood quivered as the bull scraped past. Charlie Dick pulled himself higher and the bull swung around and paced angrily beneath him.

Walt stood up and brushed the dirt from his pants. He walked to the gate that opened from the stackyard into the field and closed it to confine the bull.

"Keep a good hold on that derrick," Walt said as he swung himself onto his hayrack and untwisted the team's reins. "And be sure and look down every once in a while. Maybe you'll realize what you've been fooling with."

He shook the lines and shouted at the horses, urging them into a run. The empty rack swayed unsteadily as it rattled off over the bumps of the field.

Charlie Dick scowled after him. He felt the splintery wood of the derrick beam tearing into his bare hands and feet. Its square corners made numb lines where his knees gripped it.

A few minutes later Dad's big hay wagon came rumbling rapidly toward the stackyard with the horses at a trot. Dad pulled them to a stop at the gate and jumped down. Walt sat on the side of the wagon, smoking a cigarette. Despite the cramping ache of his muscles from clinging to the beam, Charlie Dick wondered how Walt had found that cigarette.

"Just hang on," Dad called, and carrying a large stick, he slipped through the fence.

But immediately the bull trotted toward him, and he had to retreat through the wires. Without the bull directly under him, Charlie Dick began to lower himself down the post.

"You stay there," John Hale commanded, "until we get that bull back in his pen." He turned to Walt. "We'll have to use the horses. With both of us we should be able to manage him."

He unhitched the team and pulled the harnesses from their backs. He and Walt each mounted a horse and came into the stackyard carrying large sticks. But the bull, still uncooperative, had to be whacked before the horses could crowd him across the yard and back into his pen.

Dad jumped off his horse and quickly pulled the gate shut and then handed the reins of the work bridle to Walt. "Would you take the team and hitch them up again?"

With relief Charlie Dick dropped to the ground. He stood examining his hands, where several huge splinters lay painfully embedded under the skin. When Dad came over to him, Charlie Dick held up his hands for his father to see.

"You don't need to open a gate to get through a fence, and you've no business in the bull pen anyway, the way that bull's been lately," John Hale reprimanded his son. "You ought to be whipped for opening that gate. But I guess those hands are as bad as a whipping."

"They sure are." Charlie Dick hoped for enough sympathy to escape punishment. He was a little surprised that Walt had not told Dad that he had purposefully turned the bull loose. Instead of feeling grateful, Charlie Dick was distressed to think Walt had that to hold over his head. He wished he had something like that on Walt. Perhaps the way to get rid of Walt after all would be to have something on him.

Dad still looked cross. "And your mother just brought Walt's cigarettes over to the field. Kathleen found them in a basket. You put them there, didn't you?"

"Yes, I guess I did," Charlie Dick had to admit, and he suspected that Dad was more annoyed at this than at his letting the bull out.

"Why?" he demanded.

Charlie Dick shrugged and his shoulder muscles ached from the strain of hanging on the derrick beam.

"You were going to smoke them yourself?" John Hale watched Charlie Dick closely.

"Oh, no," Charlie Dick denied in genuine surprise. "I wouldn't do that. I hate cigarettes like you and Mama do."

"Well then?"

"I just didn't want Walt smoking 'em."

Dad looked at him a moment longer. "Son, other people think different than we do. You go to the house and get those slivers out. You don't need to come back. We've already lost so much time getting the bull back in that it's too late for another load. Walt and I will handle this last one."

The boy started to leave, bothered by the turn of events. Here again he was being sent to the house while Walt, who was smugly lighting up another cigarette, stayed here to help Daddy. Charlie Dick stepped back to his father and spoke softly.

"You wouldn't fire Walt, would you?"

"Son, Walt's a good hand—the best I ever had. Smoking cigarettes is his own business. Oh, and one more thing. Miriam said that Grandpa asked her if she thought he was grumpy. She said you told him he was."

"He is awful cross," Charlie Dick replied, feeling more irritated every moment.

"He's a sick old man. When you get out those splinters, go sit with him awhile and see if you can think of something nice to say to him for a change."

Sullenly Charlie Dick trudged off toward the house.

Grandpa was wide awake when Charlie Dick went into his room later. Pulling out the splinters had been bad enough, but the iodine Mama dabbed on his sore hands still stung and added to his vexation at the failure of his tricks with the bull and the cigarettes. Instead of the hired man's being unhappy, Charlie Dick was. And Dad said he wouldn't fire Walt.

"That Walt sure thinks he's the big guy," Charlie Dick grumped as he plopped down on the chair by Grandpa's bed.

"What I want to know is where he's from? Everybody just says, 'some big city.' That ain't no answer," Grandpa commented sourly.

Charlie Dick realized he really didn't know much about Walt. If he could only find out something bad about Walt, that's all he'd need.

Grandpa was scowling and Charlie Dick in no tolerant mood scowled back. "Everybody else has already cussed me. I guess you're going to cuss me too."

Grandpa looked silently at him for a moment.

"If you are, go ahead."

"I can if you want me to," Grandpa snapped. "What is it you need to be chewed out about?"

"For telling you you're grumpy."

"You're grumpy now, and I'm telling you, so I guess we're even."

"It's because I've had such a bad day. Everything seemed to be going so good, then bam! And that's no fun when everything goes wrong."

"I know just what you mean," said Grandpa, "exactly what you mean."

"It's hard not to be cross when everything goes wrong."

"It sure is," Grandpa agreed emphatically in his old

voice, "but I guess we shouldn't be anyway. It just makes things harder for everybody around us and ourselves too. That's why I decided I'd try not to be so darned mad all the time after you told me how grumpy I was and that instead I should remember the good times I've had."

"Really, Grandpa?" Charlie Dick asked in surprise.

"Really what?" the old man snapped.

"You're really not going to be so grumpy any more?"

"Really." The old voice was milder this time. Apparently Grandpa remembered his new vow.

"Gee, that's good news." Anyway one good thing happened today, Charlie Dick thought. "And especially if you'll tell us all those good stories of what you used to do."

"Is that what you want?" Grandpa asked.

"It sure is, Grandpa. I love them stories."

"O.K. then. Maybe tonight I'll tell you how I used to haul apples in a wagon all the way to Canyon Springs to sell 'em. It was a five-day trek, and one time early in the morning of the third day . . ."

6

In annoyance Charlie Dick ripped a weed from the ground. A large bean plant came up with it. Usually if he pulled a plant by mistake, he would pat the soil back around its roots, but today he tossed it carelessly into the weed pile.

Again he was doing the girls' work. The first haying was completed, and already the new alfalfa stems were showing tall. "Walt and I are just going to brand a few calves and dehorn a couple of steers. We won't need you today," Dad had said, backing up Mama's request for Charlie Dick to help her by working in the garden.

Weeding! And when there was branding to do!

Charlie Dick scraped the weeds together and carried them to the fence. As he tossed them over, he noticed the snake on the edge of the roadway. He slipped through the wires of the fence and quickly pounced on it.

"Doggone it, it's a dead one," he said as he held it up. Then he brightened, "But it still might be useful."

A moment later Charlie Dick lay stretched out on the porch roof with his eyes just above the edge so he could see the back door. Inside he could hear the girls finishing the dishes.

As he watched, a barn cat slunk to the step and sniffed at the snake. Charlie Dick lifted on his elbows and hissed at her. She turned her head quickly and stared alertly at him with light, wide eyes. He raised his hand as though to throw a stone. The cat fled around the corner of the house.

Then Miriam was at the screen, pushing it open with the dishpan. A little of the water slopped out as she stepped down with her bare foot squarely on the body of the snake. She leaned sideways, peering around the dishpan down at her feet. Suddenly a scream seemed to propel the pan upward. It landed on the corner of the step. Water splashed inside the doorway. Miriam leaped away onto the board walk. She stood with the front of her dress hanging limply wet and water dripping down her forehead.

Kathleen trotted up to the door. "Why did you spill all that water on the floor?" She stepped out onto the snake.

Miriam pointed at the step. Kathleen did a duplicate of Miriam's performance. She howled loudly as Margaret Hale came to the door with bread dough on her hands.

"What in the world is the matter?" Then she saw the snake. "Why it's only a little dead water snake."

"But I stepped on it," Miriam shuddered, then she bristled. "I'll bet Charlie Dick put it there, Mama."

"Charlie Dick did it," Kathleen bawled. She limped over to her mother as though the foot that had touched the snake was permanently injured.

"Charlie Dick is supposed to be weeding." Margaret Hale stepped into the yard and looked toward the garden, then quickly around the yard. "All right, Charlie Dick, come down off that roof right now. I can see your hair sticking up."

Charlie Dick sat up and laughed. He barked as he slid down the roof and leaped to the ground. The crickets scattered away as he landed on all fours in the weeds.

"Charlie Dick, you go ahead and bark," Miriam sniffed, "but you're not funny."

"You get back to your weeding, Charlie Dick," Mama ordered, "and for heaven's sake, don't bother the girls any more. They still have a lot to do and now they will have to mop up that water on the floor, too."

Walt had come up the path, and when she finished scolding her son, Margaret Hale turned to him. "Would you mind getting rid of that snake for us, Walt?"

"I'll be glad to, Mrs. Hale," Walt said politely.

Charlie Dick turned toward the garden. He didn't want to watch Walt be the big hero again. As he passed Kathleen, he grimaced.

"Charlie Dick's smiling again," she cried.

Walt picked up the snake and with a long swing of his arm flung it out of the yard. "John asked that I bring Charlie Dick to help for a few minutes," Walt said to Mama. "We're having a time with those big steers."

Charlie Dick changed directions in the middle of a step and dashed toward the gate.

"Send Charlie Dick back, won't you, Walt, when you're through with him," Mama asked, "so he can work in the garden again. If we don't get some done, the weeds will take right over."

His pleasure at being needed by his father was curdled by his mother's assumption that she had claim on him full time like one of the girls, while he was only temporarily allowed with the men. And all because of Walt. He remembered his untried scheme to get something on the big man. He stopped and waited for the hired man.

"Have you ever branded before?" Charlie Dick managed a friendly tone.

"No," Walt admitted as they walked on together. "And it's tougher holding those calves than I thought it would be."

"I have—lots of times," Charlie Dick bragged. But then he remembered why he was even talking to Walt. "But I guess you weren't at your grandpa's farm all the time."

"No, I only spent a couple of summers there when I was a lot younger. Then Grandma died."

"What did you do when you weren't there?"

"Nothing much."

"Where did you live?"

"About every place. I moved around a lot."

"Did you live in big cities?"

"I always lived in big cities."

"Like Chicago?"

"Big cities like Chicago."

"What did you do? I mean after you were grown up. You must have done something for a job."

"This and that. A little of everything."

Charlie Dick was beginning to be disgusted. It was certain Walt had never done anything remotely interesting and especially nothing that could be held against him. Or else he just didn't want to talk about his past. Of all the rotten luck. His latest scheme to get rid of Walt was a complete failure.

"The Bensens had a hired man who was a clown once, and the Barns had one who used to be sailor," Charlie Dick said crossly. "I guess you ain't never been a sailor or worked in the circus?"

"Nope."

Charlie Dick leaped ahead of Walt and ran toward the corral, where his father stood waiting. What rotten luck to get a hired man who had never done nothing. Not one thing!

Charlie Dick climbed over the fence, and sat heavily on the neck of a big steer as Walt wrapped a rope around

the animal's feet and held down his rump. Dad cut at one of the struggling steer's horns with the meat saw. His nostrils trembling, the frightened animal bellowed, hideously tossing, pulling, jerking under the boy. The saw broke through and blood spurted on Charlie Dick's arm.

Walt quickly untied the steer's feet. The animal leaped up and fled to the other side of the corral. John Hale looked at his son, and Charlie Dick knew he was wondering whether that experience had been too much for a ten-year-old.

Charlie Dick held his face straight, emotionless, like a man. "That wasn't nearly as bad as weeding."

Dad patted his back before he got on the horse to catch the next steer.

That night in Grandpa's room it was companionable —the male talk of the three Hale men—Grandpa, Dad, and Charlie Dick.

"We got all the branding done today," Dad told Grandpa, "except that new calf that was born a few days ago. It's a pretty little heifer."

"I helped with the dehorning," Charlie Dick contributed. "Wow! Are those calves strong!" He rubbed a bruise on his leg where a steer's hoof had made its mark.

"You've got some good stock, John." Tonight Grandpa seemed pleased. "If you just don't lose any for a year or so, you'll have a good herd."

The warm masculine kinship tonight here in the bedroom was just the opposite of the irritation Charlie Dick had felt whenever he'd been near Walt today. However, he hadn't come in with Dad after supper just to chat aimlessly. He had something in mind. Now he tried to sound casual.

"Walt got awful tired today. I guess he's not used to working so hard. I was thinking, he might get fed up with it around here and decide to go on. I mean he's never stayed any place very long. He told me that today. So it's awful lucky you've got me to do his work in case he does go."

"Walt doesn't seem to mind hard work a bit. I don't know what I'd do without him. But you were a lot of help with those steers. I appreciate that, I'll tell you." Dad reached over and gave Charlie Dick a man-slap on the knee. Obviously Dad thought his son was fishing for a compliment, but Charlie Dick was after something bigger.

"I was thinking that we could have managed those big steers without Walt," Charlie Dick continued. "We would have just had to use a little more rope—and tied them a little better."

"Well, maybe," Dad conceded, "if we'd had to."

"In fact I could do all Walt's work. So if he does go, you don't need to worry. I'll do all his work—every bit. And you won't have to pay me as much neither. I'd save you a lot of money. I'd work the rest of the summer for just a few measly dollars."

"Well, I'll be. I think you've got the schemingest little

scamp in all Wyoming for a son." Grandpa actually smiled. "But it'd be worth a few bucks to get even part of a man's work from a ten-year-old—willing work without no guff."

"I don't claim any credit for Charlie Dick's schemes," Dad said good-naturedly. "I think he takes after his grandfather."

The two older Hales laughed lightly together. Then Dad turned to Charlie Dick. His tone was more serious. "We talked about paying you wages before, Charlie Dick. But things aren't looking as good as we'd hoped, with the locusts and all. And I don't think Walt is wanting to leave—right now at least. Still I suppose that if Walt did go, we might be able to manage a dollar or two of the cash we've been using to pay him."

Charlie Dick grinned through his freckles, and when Grandpa winked at him a moment later, he winked back. If only Walt would go . . .

After a few minutes he left the room. The girls were in the kitchen around Walt, listening to a story he was telling about getting in trouble riding cows on his Grandpa's farm when he was a boy. Even Anna was listening attentively.

"I had bruises all over me," Walt said, "but what made me sorriest was that Grandpa was mad at me because the cows wouldn't give any milk. What other people thought of me didn't matter, but I couldn't stand Grandpa to know about any trouble I was in."

"I can't imagine you ever doing anything wrong," Miriam exclaimed, making herself silly.

Kathleen giggled. "Tell us that story again."

Charlie Dick bared his teeth at her when he went by and heard her howl as he left the house.

They could sit around Walt cackling like hens that had just laid eggs if they wanted to, but Charlie Dick had better things to do.

He picked up an empty bucket from near the door and walked rapidly through the dark, moonless night to the granary, where he had discovered an abandoned nest of rotten chicken eggs several days earlier. He pulled the gunnysack off them and laid them carefully in the bucket. As he left the granary, he heard a car in the lane.

Returning to the house with the pail in his hand, he saw the door open and Walt step outside. A man followed him, and from his plump silhouette Charlie Dick was able to identify Alf, the friend who had come with Walt to the farm the first day.

Charlie Dick could tell from the sound of their voices that they were walking together toward the barnyard. He crouched in the darkness and waited.

"I didn't." Alf's voice carried to Charlie Dick. "I just came out to see you before going home. Mr. Bensen sent me in the pickup to buy some bags of feed."

Walt grunted. "You better not be gone too long with it."

Charlie Dick wondered that Walt didn't sound very happy to see Alf. Why, if his friend Dan Barns came out to see Charlie Dick, he'd sure be glad.

"Now what's bothering you?" Walt continued. "We can talk in private out here."

They stepped within arm's length of Charlie Dick, then moved on by.

That's what you think, Charlie Dick said silently to himself.

"I'm tired of being in this dull place." Alf's voice was sarcastic. "Imagine me, Big Alf, feeding the piggie wiggies and gathering the eggs from the chickie wickies."

"It don't seem so bad to me. In fact I like it here better than any place we've been." Walt gave a little laugh. "I'm as contented as a baby."

Charlie Dick was dismayed to learn that all his tricks on Walt hadn't dented his liking for the Hale place.

"And you ought to be glad for the hard work—to slim you down some."

Alf ignored Walt's last comment and said in his complaining tone, "Working our heads off. That don't seem like contentment to me. Carrying heavy buckets and pitching hay with dirt falling back in our eyes. I'm looking for something easier. I think there might be a job at a place in Hanging Rock—a man named Stone."

"In Hanging Rock?" asked Walt in a tone of disbelief.

"Yup, in Hanging Rock."

I've got the means to dampen Walt's contentment right here in the bucket, Charlie Dick thought, and the only thing better than one target is two. With one as big as Alf I won't waste a egg.

But he wouldn't rush in and use up his eggs right off. First he would give Walt a run for his money. Charlie Dick had wanted to make another dummy ever since that day he made one in Grandpa's room. Now all he needed was a rope and some gunnysacks. The eggs could be the climax.

He dashed through the darkness to the toolshed and quickly found the necessary items. Then stripping off his shirt and pants, he stuffed them with gunnysacks. A folded, stuffed bag made a head. He tied a rope to the back straps of the overalls and steadied the head with a piece of wire threaded through the burlap. He hurried in his underwear through the darkness back to the chicken coop. In a moment he was scooting with his dummy and eggs up the clay coop roof with its one-way slope that ended high above the heads of the two farm hands.

Cautiously Charlie Dick peered over the edge of the roof. In the darkness he could just make out the two men squatted below him, talking quietly.

With the rope Charlie Dick slowly lowered the dummy over the edge around the corner from the men. When he felt the dummy touch the ground, he maneuvered it to where it would be partly visible to Walt and Alf.

"Hey, what was that?" Alf suddenly asked.

Charlie Dick jerked the dummy back from view.

"What?" Walt asked.

"I thought I saw something move there by the corner. I guess I'm seeing things. Anyway I want to check on that job. Hey, there it is again!" He jumped up.

Hand over hand Charlie Dick swiftly pulled on the rope. The clothes scraped the roof edge as he jerked them up.

At the sound Walt stood up and walked to the corner. He peered through the darkness along the side.

"It's that cockeyed kid! He's always up to something." He moved back to Alf and stooped down again.

"I don't like being spied on," Alf stated.

"Me either, but that boy is just the one who'd eavesdrop," Walt replied.

"He'd better not come back," grunted Alf.

"He'll be back. I'll bet on that."

"When he comes, I'll catch him and box his ears," Alf growled.

Charlie Dick smothered a chuckle before he crawled silently to the other corner, the one the men weren't watching. There he lowered the dummy and moved it out into view. When they didn't notice, he tossed down a pebble from the roof. Both men swung toward the noise.

"There he is!"

Alf sprang to his feet and dashed to the corner, but Charlie Dick already had the dummy up with him.

"That kid can sure run fast. You go this way and I'll go that." Alf puffed off.

Walt started in the other direction.

Charlie Dick stretched himself out next to the dummy to escape being seen as they trotted around the low slope of the roof.

"You didn't see him either?" Alf asked when they met. "Then he's gotta be hiding somewhere."

Charlie Dick felt so confident that he jiggled the rope as they came around the corner, and the dummy did a dance, its trouser legs rustling the dried weeds.

"There he is!"

"You're faster than me. I'll wait here and you chase him around to me," Alf spoke softly. As Walt rushed off, Alf threatened, "I'll get you this time."

Charlie Dick peered over the edge and watched Alf try to flatten his big form against the wall. Soon Walt's running steps approached from the other direction.

"Now I got you." Alf leaped at Walt in the darkness.

All Charlie Dick could see of the two men was a black tangle on the ground. Confused cursing came from it. This was the opportunity Charlie Dick had been waiting for. He pulled the bucket near him, scooped out an egg with each hand and sent them flying. The crisp sound of the eggs cracking was followed by the fetid odor.

"What in the . . . ?"

The swearing increased. Charlie Dick continued to pepper the eggs downward. The jumble on the ground had untangled into two separate shapes as he pulled the last eggs from the bucket. He jumped to his feet in full view.

"He's up on the . . ."

Charlie Dick sent the last of the ammunition down with the force of a hardball pitcher.

". . . roof. Ugh!"

Then holding his nose against the rank smell and barking his loudest, Charlie Dick ran down the roof, leaped to the ground, dashed past the woodpile and hid safely on the far side of the coalshed. Elated with the success of his trick, he laughed quietly to himself and then turned to listen to the searching activities at the coop.

"What in the . . . ?"

"It's only a dummy," Walt exclaimed.

"When I get my hands on that kid . . ."

"Forget the boy. Let's get this stuff off," Walt's voice said.

Charlie Dick waited until he heard them at the flowing well before he slipped around to the porch. Gee, that had been a good one—the best one yet, the very best. Charlie Dick chuckled. It was too bad, however, he reflected, that Walt wasn't as interested in a job in town as Alf, especially while Dad had enough cash left to pay Charlie Dick something. Maybe if he kept hounding Walt . . .

7

Charlie Dick sat on the floor in the kitchen struggling to tug on his last year's school shoes. His clean bib overalls had both hooks on them, and his socks matched. As he loosened the laces, he was hoping that he would be able to find Dan Barns as soon as they arrived in town so he wouldn't waste any precious time. The Fourth of July was always the best day all summer.

"We appreciate you driving the kids into Hanging Rock." Dad stood with his hand on the screen door ready to start for the east field. "Besides, you deserve a day off. You've put in some pretty full ones lately." He shook Walt's hand before he left the house.

Walt's hair was slicked down and his shirt collar buttoned. He turned to Mama. "I wanted to go. Alf's expecting me to meet him."

"We're glad to have you drive the children into town.

You're as much help to us, Walt, as if you'd fallen straight out of heaven," Mama replied.

Charlie Dick stood up in the tight shoes, wondering if he could stand them on for the whole day.

"I'm glad you're taking us," Kathlen giggled excitedly to Walt, and Miriam nodded in agreement as she put sandwiches in a paper bag. She hardly looked like herself with her hair combed neatly back from her face.

Charlie Dick ignored the two girls' open admiration of the hired man. Then Anna, her delicate face flushed with excitement, smiled at Walt too. Well, Walt wouldn't look so big and important to Anna when she had her little doll in her hands from Charlie Dick. And he knew just how he'd get it.

He left the kitchen at a run and was almost to the woodpile before Miriam came out the door with the lunch sack. "Charlie Dick, come back here," she called. "We're ready to leave now."

"I'll be right back," he answered over his shoulder. He ran past the chicken coop, through the barnyard, and straight to the toolshed.

The small silver spurs with the etched star designs were hanging on a nail under the bridles. He pulled the bridles off them and lifted them down. In his hand, the metal gleamed and the rowels spun easily. He dropped them quickly in a gunny sack and raced back to the pickup.

"It's about time you got back here, Charlie Dick," Miriam nagged as he leaped over the side.

He dropped the sack in the corner as Walt started the motor. They drove out of the yard, but Miriam didn't ask Charlie Dick what was in the sack.

"If you've made us late for the parade, I'll . . . I'll scream," she continued her annoyed fretting.

"We won't be late," he told Miriam in an even tone.

When Anna, in the cab, turned around and smiled out the back window at him, he grinned. When he winked, she winked back.

But he did feel a little guilty. He placed his foot on the gunnysack to keep the spurs from bouncing around. Quickly he reassured himself. Hadn't Uncle Henry's gift of the spurs two years earlier been to the whole family? Wasn't Charlie Dick a member of the family? And weren't they too small for Dad's big shoes? Since Charlie Dick was the only boy, they would be his. It was true Mama had worn them a couple of times last summer when she went riding with Daddy, but she hadn't even been on a horse this year. Yes, his plan was a good one, Charlie Dick decided. Since the spurs were practically his anyway, he would use them to get the money to buy the doll for Anna.

"I don't hear any drums," Miriam said when the pickup reached the outskirts of Hanging Rock.

But as they passed Bee's Store on Main Street, almost

the whole population of Hanging Rock and the surrounding farm country was lined up on the sidewalks. Charlie Dick stuck out his chest and saluted first left then right like a general returned from the war. They reached the show house and Walt turned the truck into a side street and pulled it to a stop in the shade of some large poplar trees.

Charlie Dick purposely waited until his sisters were out of the pickup before he climbed down from the back. Walt was in front of him, sauntering unexcitedly after the girls. Charlie Dick quickly pulled the small square, torn from an old sheet, from his pocket and shook it out. He chuckled at the hastily penciled words on it.

KICK ME

Holding it by the upper corners where he had stuck pieces of Dad's black friction tape, he ran into Walt's back. Then he dodged out around him. The sign stuck.

"Oh, sorry about that," he said in mock humility, then he ran ahead to join his sisters.

Drums began beating at the school two blocks away. Charlie Dick found a place in front of the show house, where the crowd was thinner. They were mostly grownups and didn't complain when he slipped in front of them. He grabbed Anna's hand and pulled her up near him. Miriam and Kathleen followed. Walt stood behind with the other adults. Charlie Dick glanced back, but the people around Walt seemed not to have noticed the sign

on his back. Charlie Dick hoped no one would tell him about it before some of the junior high boys saw it. That was just the sort of thing they would have a big time with. As the drums grew louder, several girls crowded in near the Hale children. They hugged Miriam and exclaimed over how they hadn't seen her all summer. The men in the crowd took off their hats as Charlie Dick saw the first of the parade—several men of the American Legion each carrying a United States flag. Charlie Dick hopped on one foot and then the other in his tight shoes. He grinned down at Anna. Her small face was beautifully radiant.

Through the milling crowd Charlie Dick looked for Walt. He was nowhere close and the boy decided he must have left before the parade was over. Charlie Dick thought it too bad that he would miss seeing the fulfillment of his joke.

Some of the children who had watched the parade were now out in the street gathering up bits of crepe paper that had been lost from floats. Charlie Dick was tempted to join them but decided that first of all he must find Dan Barns.

Miriam was already walking away with her friends. "You watch Anna and Kathleen, Charlie Dick," she called back over her shoulder.

"I will not," Charlie Dick argued. "That's your job."

"I want to go with Miriam," Kathleen sobbed.

"All right, come on then." Miriam stopped long enough for Kathleen to catch up before she went giggling her way up the sidewalk with the crowd of girls.

"Come on, Anna," Charlie Dick said as he started across the street. Miriam, he thought, could just as well have taken Anna too. As much as he loved Anna, still it was a hard thing to have your little sister with you in town on the Fourth of July.

The streets were crowded with horses and floats returning from the south side of town where the parade ended. Anna's eyes had been open, wondering, during the parade, but now she kept them down.

"You don't need to be scared, Anna. Nobody will hurt you."

She clung tightly to her brother's arm as they dodged between the groups of people.

"Charlie Dick!"

He swung around.

Dan Barns ran toward him from behind two band members who were, between them, carrying the school's big bass horn.

"I was hoping you would be in town today."

"Hi, Dan," Charlie Dick grinned. "I've been looking for you."

They ducked back against the wall of Bee's Store as a large group of band members strode by.

"Let's go up to the park. Russ Jones and those other sissy guys are there. Me and you can stand 'em all and still win."

100

"O.K.," Charlie Dick agreed enthusiastically.

He turned, jerking free from Anna's hand in his haste, and started back up the street. Then he stopped and looked around at his little sister huddled against the store wall.

"Have you got to *tend* your little sister?" Dan asked almost accusingly.

"Nope," Charlie Dick replied loudly, but before he went on up the street with Dan, he called, "Anna, you find Miriam, or if you want, go back to the truck. You know where the truck is." He paused a moment. "And I'll have something for you on the way home." He turned and dashed after Dan around the corner. "I'll race you to the school."

Dan was way behind when Charlie Dick passed the school building and ran onto the big football field. He was busily picking up soft drink bottle caps when Dan caught up with him.

"Get some ammunition!" he ordered, dumping a handful of the caps into the side pocket of his bib overalls.

Running toward the bleachers a moment later, he and Dan screamed like Apaches and slung caps at a group of boys near the top. They immediately retreated behind the football field to the picnic area where the tall poplar trees shaded the scanty grass and dirty tables.

Charlie Dick ran to the top of the bleachers and signaled his triumph by clasping his hands together above his head boxer style.

"I'm the boss of Bunker Hill." He sang out the words

as a challenge to the backs of all the retreating army.

It was afternoon when Charlie Dick ran toward Bee's Store swinging the gunnysack that held the spurs. Dan Barns trotted along at his heels.

"I thought my family was going to eat the big lunch we brought up by the football field, but they sure didn't come up there."

"They probably ate without you just like my family without me," Charlie Dick suggested.

When he had taken the spurs from the pickup a few minutes earlier, he'd seen that the huge lunch sack was gone. That was O.K. Charlie Dick didn't mind so much missing lunch but something about the little lone Anna asleep on the pickup seat made him miserable.

He should have taken her up to the park with him, he reflected. She could have sat in the corner by the fence and watched. She never was in the way. But he would give her the doll on the way home and everything would be all right again, he told himself.

"My breadbasket is sure empty," Dan complained, holding his stomach.

They leaped up the concrete steps and pushed open one of the worn double doors into Bee's Store.

"I'm kind of hungry myself."

The two boys had to zigzag through the crowded aisles. They were held up by a group of girls with ice cream cones, and Charlie Dick had time to look nonchalantly at the dolls displayed on the wall shelves. A tiny doll on the lowest shelf was tied into her small white box. Her hair was blond. Charlie Dick was sure she would do for Anna. When he squinted, he could just make out the price. Two dollars.

"Hey, Charlie Dick, that one is two dollars," Dan exclaimed at his elbow.

Charlie Dick turned toward Dan, wondering how his friend had known he was looking at the doll, but Dan pointed through the glass top of the nearest counter at a black pocketknife displayed on a dirty piece of blue taffeta.

"I'd sure like that," Dan said.

The gang of girls moved out of their path, so the boys continued on.

"Me too! Grandpa's got a pocketknife twice that big. It's got five blades and a can opener."

They stopped in front of the candy counter where Mr. Bee was dipping up a pound of horehound. They had to wait in line for a while before he looked at Charlie Dick.

"What for you?"

"First, I want two pennies' worth of bubble gum." Charlie Dick fished the pennies from his pocket and dropped them on the rubber money mat on the counter. "And then I want to sell you these."

He pulled the spurs from the gunnysack and held them up. The rowels spun around with a jingle.

"Sorry, I don't handle used stuff," Mr. Bee said as he put four pieces of gum in Charlie Dick's hand.

"But they've hardly been used, and they're just like new. I only want to trade them to you for something that costs two dollars. You can see they're worth a lot more than two dollars."

"Sorry, boy, but I just can't handle used stuff. Why, if I did it once, everybody in the valley would be hauling their junk in here." He turned away from Charlie Dick toward Dan. "What for you?"

"Nothing." Dan shook his head and backed up.

"Doggone it," Charlie Dick grumbled as they pushed their way back out of the crowded store. He tucked the spurs under his arm, and the boys stood together on the corner as Charlie Dick shared the gum. "Doggone it," he complained, "my bubble gum fortunes are both the same. They both say, 'You are on the crossroads of opportunity.'"

Just then an older boy ran toward them from across the street. "Dan Barns, where have you been?" Steve Barns frowned down on his little brother. "Mom said she'll skin you for running off so long. We've got to go home. You'd better get back to the truck."

"Already?" Dan asked, gnawing on the hard gum.

Steve clutched his shoulder to lead him off.

Charlie Dick took the spurs from under his arm and looked at their lovely shining metal. "You'd think Mr. Bee would jump at the chance to get these for two dollars."

104

"Maybe Jake's Hardware will buy them." Dan spoke with gum bulging one cheek. "They have lots of spurs, and some of 'em are used too."

Steve stopped pulling on Dan's arm and asked, "What spurs are you selling? Let me see them."

Charlie Dick handed them to the bigger boy. Steve turned them slowly in his hands.

"They're almost new and look at that pretty star pattern on the side."

Steve pulled the short leather straps off, then fitted them back on.

"You can see they ain't worn a bit."

Steve bent down and slipped them on the back of his heels. "You say you want two dollars for them?"

"Yup, only two dollars. They're worth lots more. You can see that."

Looking over his shoulder down at the spurs on his feet, Steve considered a moment longer.

"They sure do fit good," Charlie Dick urged.

"Yes, they do. Maybe I'll take them. They're just what I need."

"Do you have two dollars?" Dan blurted out.

Steve looked down his nose at his little brother. "Sure, I've got two dollars." As he stooped to pull the spurs from his shoes, he spoke up at Charlie Dick. "I've got two dollars home from helping Mr. Bensen, but Dad will lend me two until I get home. I'll bring it right back to you. Come on now, Dan." Steve grasped his brother's arm and half dragged him up the street.

While he waited for Steve to come back, Charlie Dick went in the store again to look at the doll but spent most of the time examining the pocketknife as thoroughly as possible through the thick glass. He expected to find Steve on the sidewalk when he came out, but Steve was nowhere in sight. Charlie Dick sat on the curb chewing his bubble gum until it was as flavorless as warm water from the tea kettle. But Steve didn't come.

So, watching carefully for him, Charlie Dick walked slowly up Main Street. At the corner he looked toward the high school. The Barns's truck was not in front of the building where it had been earlier.

Charlie Dick was puzzled and a little disturbed. Steve surely wouldn't steal the spurs, would he? Oh, no. Steve wouldn't do a thing like that. Charlie Dick pushed the thought from his mind, but it lingered near, probably because he himself did not feel right about having taken the spurs from home.

"Charlie Dick!"

The boy spun around. However it wasn't Steve who had called.

Walt strode toward him closely followed by Alf. "Charlie Dick, I've been looking for you."

Charlie Dick backed away, keeping just out of reach of the big man. Walt wouldn't be happy about that "Kick Me" sign.

"Why have you been looking for me? Is it time to go home?" Charlie Dick asked innocently.

"In a while, but we got a little job for you."

106

"And it will be worth a couple of bucks to you next week when we come in on Founders' Day," contributed Alf, who looked very friendly for the first time.

"Two dollars? Then I'll do it." Charlie Dick allowed the two men to come near him. "But ain't you mad about that sign?"

"No," Walt said good-naturedly. "For a while I couldn't figure out why those boys kept sneaking up behind me and giving me a kick. Then it dawned on me that I must have a sign on my back. I used to play that very same trick when I was a kid."

"You did?" Charlie Dick asked, hardly believing that Walt could ever have teased anyone and disappointed that the joke he'd thought so clever was known far and wide.

"You see, Charlie Dick," Walt continued. "We heard that Mr. Stone is looking for a gardener. You know who Mr. Stone is, don't you?"

"Yes," Charlie Dick said, then informed them, "he's awful rich and everybody calls him Old Stoneheart because he's so grumpy."

"Alf here doesn't like farm work very much."

"It's not my kind of work," Alf added.

"So we were thinking that it might be a good job for him. But he can't ask himself 'cause word might get back to the Bensens and he'd lose his job there."

Charlie Dick nodded, but he wished it were Walt who was considering the job instead of Alf.

"What we want you to do," said Walt, "is go there and

ask him about the job for us. Ask him what the garden-er's duties would be, how much he'd pay and how much time he'd get off, if he'd get off on weekends and holidays."

"I can do that easy," said Charlie Dick confidently.

"Fine," concluded Walt. "We'll meet you back here in a few minutes."

Charlie Dick started off at a run.

"Be sure and find out about time off on holidays," Alf called after him.

Charlie Dick asked Mr. Stone all the questions he'd been told to and although the old man had finally said he didn't need a gardener, Alf and Walt seemed pleased with Charlie Dick's information when he returned. That is the easiest two dollars I've ever earned, Charlie Dick thought as he and the two men walked together toward the pickup.

The girls were waiting when they arrived. Miriam was chattering about how she and her friends had talked some of the boys who had horses and a wagon made into a float to give them a long tour of the town.

Kathleen beside her said, "I got to ride too." She looked pretty tired.

Anna stood quietly on the running board by the open pickup door. Her dress was wrinkled and her hair was pressed to one side where she had lain on the pickup seat asleep. Her thin arms hung limply at her sides. Her expressionless face and the dullness of her eyes told of her disappointment in the day that had promised so much.

Charlie Dick felt her misery. He slipped the two fortunes from his bubble gum into her hand. He wished he'd saved the gum too. If he only had the doll to give her. Yet he knew that her disappointment was not only in the doll. Again he had let her down. He watched her standing so motionless, so lifeless, and he vowed solemnly to himself that he wouldn't disappoint her or be unkind to her again. And on Founders' Day he would get the doll. Walt would pay him then, and the family usually came to town for the afternoon program at the park when Old Mr. Stone himself always gave a speech. For certain there would be no slipup this time.

"We better be going now," Walt told the children. "We shouldn't have waited until so late. It'll be dark before we get home now."

"Then it's settled?" Alf asked Walt. "That program next week starts at 3:30. I'll meet you then."

Walt hesitated for a moment. "I don't know."

"I intend to use my opportunities." Annoyance grated Alf's voice.

"You are on the crossroads of opportunity," Charlie Dick quoted the fortunes.

Walt gave him a suspicious look as though he expected a new trick, then he stepped into the pickup. "O.K. Alf. I'll meet you at 3:30."

John and Margaret Hale were sitting in the kitchen when Charlie Dick pushed the door open ahead of his sisters. John Hale lifted Elizabeth Eliza down from his knee, where he had been giving her a pony ride, and stood up.

"Charlie Dick, what have you been up to?" The tone was serious, not a have-you-been-teasing-again tone.

Miriam fell silent from her giggling chatter. Even Walt stopped in the doorway with the screen half open.

"Why, nothing," Charlie Dick denied.

He glanced at Mama's pained face, then followed her eyes across the room. On the very center of the table with the star designs twinkling in the artificial light lay the small silver spurs.

Charlie Dick gulped and looked back at his father.

"Steve Austin came by with two dollars for you. We kept the spurs instead." Dad's brows were tight together.

"You see," Charlie Dick began, "I was going to get . . ." but he stopped. He wouldn't make Anna feel bad again. That promise to himself he'd keep.

Everyone was staring at him except Mama, whose eyes were down. She looked so miserable and Anna so worried that Charlie Dick tried again.

"We never used 'em, and . . ." Somehow his rationalization of this morning that the spurs were his anyway now didn't seem so sound.

Dad walked over to him and tilted his chin up so he had to look straight at him. "You know that is stealing, don't you?"

Miriam gave a short, hysterical laugh. Kathleen started to sniffle. Anna was quiet.

110

"I guess so," Charlie Dick had to admit.

"And you know it's wrong?"

"I guess so." Charlie Dick swallowed hard, trying to keep down the sick feeling that was rising in him. Even Walt stared at him silently.

"Have you taken anything else?" John Hale asked. His eyes shot out searching arrows.

"Oh, no." Charlie Dick almost added sir, although he had never addressed his father like that.

"What about the next time?"

"Next time?" Charlie Dick asked, but his voice shook.

"It's always easier the next time."

"Never." He was glad Dad looked away for a moment toward Mama.

"You've never done it before and you won't ever again." Dad unbuckled his belt. "That means I've just got to punish you for this once."

He took Charlie Dick's shoulder and they walked around his big-eyed sisters. Walt opened the screen door. They stepped outside into the darkness.

Later lying on his stomach on his cot Charlie Dick's throat ached as much as his back from choking down the tears and remorse. He wished Walt hadn't been there to witness the scene in the kitchen and he wished now Walt were not in the porch sitting on his cot in the darkness, silently smoking a cigarette. Charlie Dick turned on his side so he could see the bright white star just now above the horizon, and as he relaxed the tight control over himself, an involuntary sob made a jerking sound in his throat.

"Anyway your pa cares what you do," Walt said.

Charlie Dick tried to ignore the big man he disliked so much.

"He wouldn't have whipped you if he didn't care."

Charlie Dick could hear Walt grinding the cigarette butt under his shoe on the concrete floor.

"My pa never cared one smidgen what I did. Not one smidgen."

8

"Are you about through?" Charlie Dick asked, now sure that he had made a mistake by consenting to Miriam's scheme.

"How do you think I can finish putting this lipstick on you if you're talking?" Miriam moaned. She leaned over Charlie Dick as he sat on the kitchen chair Kathleen had pushed into Grandpa's room for them. "There, rub your lips together."

"Are you sure your ma wants you using her lipstick and powder and stuff?" Grandpa asked.

"She doesn't care," Miriam replied, "does she, Anna?"

Anna looked up from the floor where she had her cardboard doll furniture arranged, but she didn't agree as quickly with Miriam as she always did with Charlie Dick.

If Mama did care, she couldn't blame Charlie Dick, for the oldest one home was always in charge, and Miriam was boss today.

"I'm not sitting here much longer," Charlie Dick prodded his older sister, who was drawing thin lines over the heavy powder with an eyebrow pencil.

At noon after Mama, Daddy, and Walt had left, Charlie Dick looked at the dishes he was supposed to help with and suggested they play mumblety-peg out in the yard. He had yielded to Miriam's countersuggestion that they paint him up like a lady only after Anna had reminded them that Mama told them not to leave the house while Elizabeth Eliza was asleep for her nap. But Miriam was so slow with the painting job that now Charlie Dick was restless. He was glad, however, that he had insisted they come in Grandpa's room. Charlie Dick was grateful to Grandpa.

"It ain't so important that you did something wrong. What's important is what you learned from it," Grandpa had told him the day after the Fourth of July celebration.

"I sure learned not to take anything ever again no matter what," Charlie Dick said.

He didn't know why he'd told Grandpa about taking the spurs in the first place, but he was glad he had.

"Even your pa had to learn that when he was little. He took your Grandma's eggs and traded 'em for jelly beans."

"He did?' Charlie Dick asked, surprised that his sturdy, upright father had ever stepped out of line.

"It wasn't so bad what he done, but I figgered honesty begins at home, so I walloped him good. I guess that was

114

the only time he ever took anything," Grandpa had finished.

So whether Grandpa enjoyed the makeup fun or not, at least it was something to keep his mind off the crickets.

"They've got two of them canvas rigs with poison in 'em?" Grandpa asked.

"Yes," Charlie Dick assured him. "And Mama's gone to town for some more poison. Dad took the canvas off the combine to loop down behind the bar for the crickets to fall into, and then late last night he put the second rig together from that old rake behind the barn." He added a little bitterly, "I could have helped him, but Walt did. They sent me to bed."

"Honestly, Charlie Dick, you're moving around awful," Miriam said.

"I wish I was way over there in the east field driving the rig in Walt's place instead of sitting here all dolled up," Charlie Dick argued, wishing he would get a really important job for a change. "Dad said maybe when Mama gets back I can help shovel the poisoned crickets into the wagon when the rig gets to the end of the field."

The old man had lifted his head from his pillow, but now he sank back onto it. "It beats the way we used to have to fight 'em. When the years was bad, we didn't get no crop at all. Sometimes the wheat was all gone by the middle of July; then we'd dig up some fields and put potatoes in so we'd have something to eat in the winter."

"Now all we've got to do is tie this towel around his head in a turban—like Mrs. Bensen wears to church," Miriam said, folding the towel on her knee.

Grandpa was still in the same line of thought. "We'd get the longest rope we could find—Henry and me, each on one end. Henry was my big brother, and we'd pull it tight and then walk through the wheat field hour after hour holding the rope just so high. The rope would knock the crickets off the stalks. The devils climb up and bite the heads off, then jump back to the ground for a feast. Pretty soon you've got a fine field of wheat still standing with not a head left on."

"Gee, that sounds fun!" Charlie Dick jumped up from the chair even though Miriam complained that the turban stuck out funny on one side. "That little field behind the granary has got oats in it. I'll get a rope from the toolshed." At least this would get him out of the house.

"You can't go," Miriam bossed. "We just got you all pretty." She cocked her head to one side. "Isn't he pretty! He should have been a girl. Doesn't he make a pretty girl?"

"He is pretty," Anna agreed from the floor.

Even Grandpa smiled at Charlie Dick's altered appearance.

"You look just like Aunt Rosey," Kathleen put in.

"He does," Miriam agreed. "We've got Aunt Rosey here today."

"Phooey. I'm going to get this dumb girl stuff off and

go knock the locusts off them oat stalks. You'll hold one end of the rope, Anna, won't you?"

Anna nodded.

"Aunt Rosey, Aunt Rosey," Miriam sang.

But she was interrupted by a loud knock.

Miriam and Kathleen dashed into the living room. Charlie Dick hobbled along after them as rapidly as the high heels would allow. Miriam was already holding open the screen.

"Oh, hi, Dan. Come in."

Dan Barns stepped into the house and looked around.

Oh, no, Charlie Dick thought, the one time Dan comes out to see me all summer, and I have to be dolled up like this. I'll never hear the end of it. But it was too late to hide, for Dan was looking straight at Charlie Dick. But he didn't laugh or sneer or anything. He just turned back to Miriam.

"Is Charlie Dick around?"

Miriam squeaked a sudden short laugh.

When Dan looked puzzled, she regained her composure and replied, "No, he's gone, but you haven't ever met our Aunt Rosey, have you?"

Again Dan looked toward Charlie Dick. "No, I guess not."

Kathleen began giggling, and Dan looked down at his clothes to see if he had a hole in them in an embarrassing place. Charlie Dick was relieved that Dan didn't recognize him in this humiliating costume. He pulled his throat up tight and spoke in a high precise voice, not unlike the real Aunt Rosey.

"How do you do?"

Dan glanced back up. "Hi." His voice was flat, and he looked very uncomfortable when the girls snickered. "It's too bad Charlie Dick's not here."

"Yes," said Aunt Rosey with a straight face, "too bad he's not here. He's my favorite of all my nieces and nephews."

"Aunt Rosey don't really like Charlie Dick the best, does she?" Kathleen asked.

"Well, I guess I'd better be going." Dan said, backing out the door.

"I hope we meet again," Charlie Dick intoned.

Dan gave a weak nod through the partly open screen door, then dropped it suddenly and spun away at a run. Miriam now screamed with laughter. Proud of the cleverness of his impersonation, Charlie Dick laughed too. But at the same time he regretted having missed the chance to play with Dan—and all because of that silly Miriam. He kicked off the shoes, pulled the towel from his hair, and began wiping at the makeup.

"Come on, Anna," he said, "me and you are going to fix them locusts." He pulled off the bathrobe and tossed it to the floor as Anna joined him from the bedroom.

"Pull the rope tight," Grandpa called after them, "and be sure you don't drag it too low or you'll break the stalks. Pull it so you just knock the heads."

"O.K., Grandpa."

Charlie Dick motioned to Anna. She followed as he trotted into the kitchen. He would show Daddy what a fine worker he was. Then if Walt did decide to go off to another job in Hanging Rock with Alf, Dad would be pleased to pay him some of Walt's wages.

"Charlie Dick, come back here and put up these clothes and towel you were wearing," Miriam called after him.

"You girls put them up," Charlie Dick countered as he pushed open the screen and dashed outside. "You're the ones who drug them out."

"And you haven't done the dishes yet."

He hurriedly splashed cold water from the flowing well on his face to remove the makeup and was passing the woodpile when Miriam threw open the screen and shouted after him.

"Come back here and help us. And we need Anna."

Kathleen, beside her, added, "You have to do it. Miriam's boss while Mama's gone."

Anna hesitated. "Maybe we should finish the dishes first," she worried, but when her brother gave her a come-on nod, she followed.

"We'll tell Mama if you don't."

Charlie Dick wasn't going to stand around and be nagged at by a bunch of girls. He kept going just as if he couldn't hear.

The oat heads were beginning to turn yellow, but the

stalks were still supple enough to spring back straight after the rope passed. At first Charlie Dick had whopped at the scattering crickets as he walked through the field. But now he only strode forward, sometimes wiping the sweat from his forehead and sometimes calling to Anna to pull up the slack in the rope.

When they came to the fence at the end of the field, Charlie Dick walked over to Anna.

"You gotta keep up, Anna, and pull the rope tighter." But immediately he wished he hadn't said it, for she looked forlorn as she stared at the end of the rope that dangled from her limp arms.

"You're tired, aren't you?" he asked sympathetically.

His little sister nodded.

"Let's sit down and rest a minute. When we cool off, we won't be so tired."

He parted the wires of the fence and ducked between, careful of the barbs, then held his foot on the wire for Anna to follow. They sat on the bank of the empty irrigation ditch in the alfalfa field, and Charlie Dick dug mud from the bottom of the ditch and slapped it onto his face.

"Gee, that feels good. You ought to try it. It feels like snow on my face."

But now as the sun shone hot on his head, Charlie Dick could hardly remember the feel of the cold snow of last winter. He wiggled his toes down into the mud, but the murmuring rustle of insects among the growth around him made him anxious to get back to work.

"Are you ready to go again, Anna?" he asked. He held the wires of the fence apart for her to crawl through.

She stood up slowly, and he knew she was still tired. As much as he wanted to continue his war against the crickets, still he wouldn't make Anna keep on working. He'd go back to the house and get Kathleen. She would bawl the whole time she helped him, but she was stronger than Anna.

His little sister suddenly pointed across the irrigation ditch. "Is that Old Buttons?" she asked.

Charlie Dick turned. Where the land lowered near the gate, the white hide of a cow showed above the tall greenery. A black circle with four white dots not unlike a button stood out clearly on her back.

"Yes, that's Buttons. But how did she get here in the alfalfa patch?"

"Do you think we'd better get her out," Anna asked timidly, "before she tramps down too much alfalfa?"

"She won't hurt the alfalfa. But the stupid old thing will get herself a whopper of a bellyache."

Charlie Dick started along the fence toward the cow. Anna followed, dragging the rope behind. As Charlie Dick walked in front of her to open the gate, Buttons backed away. He threw the wire gate aside, but stopped after turning back to the cow.

"Anna, does that cow look all right to you?"

Anna was staring at Buttons too. "She's awful fat."

"The stupid thing. She's probably been in the field a

long time. The fence must be down somewheres."

"Is she bloated?" Anna asked anxiously.

"She don't look good to me. You'd think she'd know when to stop eating. But cows has got different stomachs from ours, and if all that green hay swells up . . ." Again Charlie Dick measured Buttons' swollen middle with his eyes. "We'd better not let her get any water or that'll be the end of her. The first thing she'll head for is the watering trough. You bring her, Anna, and I'll run on to the yards and head her off from the trough so we can drive her into the barn."

Charlie Dick spun around and trotted up the lane. After he'd left the gateway, Buttons came out of the field of her own accord walking as rapidly as her fat stomach would allow. Anna came along behind.

Charlie Dick stationed himself in front of the watering trough near the cowbarn door. Buttons' feet crumbled some dry clods as she came nearer, her nose out to the water.

"Hoy, get in there, Buttons." Charlie Dick jumped up and down waving his arms.

The cow tried to dodge around him, but Charlie Dick kept right in front of her, adding a couple of war whoops whenever she attempted some new tactic. When Anna joined him, they gradually crowded her into the barn. Charlie Dick pulled the door shut behind her.

"Come on, Anna, we better go to the house and tell Mama what that stupid Buttons has done—that is if she's home yet."

The pickup wasn't in the yard, but Charlie Dick ran into the kitchen and demanded anyway, "Where's Mama?"

"She isn't back yet, and it's about time you came back in here, Charlie Dick and helped us," Miriam bossed as she spooned some peas into Elizabeth Eliza's mouth.

"Buttons has been into the green hay, and she's all swollen up."

Kathleen looked like she was going to cry.

But Miriam just sneered at Charlie Dick in her superior way. "Don't pay any attention to Charlie Dick. He's just trying to scare us with his teases."

But Kathleen started to sniffle. "I wish Mama was here. What if there wasn't any poison left in Hanging Rock and she had to go all the way to White City? She said she might."

"I am not teasing," Charlie Dick argued. When Anna came in the kitchen, he asked, "Buttons *has* been into the alfalfa, hasn't she, Anna?"

Anna nodded, but Miriam kept shoving the peas at Elizabeth Eliza, an even expression on her face. "Anna always agrees with Charlie Dick, no matter what. I'm not going to fret over nothing Charlie Dick says."

"Dumb girls." In disgust Charlie Dick strode past them into the living room. "I'm glad Grandpa's here."

"Grandpa's asleep and don't you go waking him over any of your silly teases," Miriam ordered.

But Charlie Dick went straight to Grandpa's room. He stopped at the side of the bed and looked down at the

124

closed eyelids clearly showing the impressions of the eyeballs underneath.

"Grandpa," he whispered, "are you asleep?"

The gray lashes flickered.

"You aren't asleep, are you, Grandpa?"

The old eyes blinked a couple of times.

"Buttons got into the green hay and she's started to swell up."

New life came into the tired eyes.

"And Mama's not back. Maybe I better run over to the east field and get Daddy."

"That's a long jaunt, and a cow could die in the time it takes you. Did she get any water?"

"No, me and Anna wouldn't let her. We put her in the barn. But I could run all the way to the east field."

"Send one of the girls for your pa if you want, but you'd better stay here. There ain't no one else around here that's got the nerve to take care of a bloated cow except you." He lifted a bony hand and looked at it. "And me, and I can't. Is the cow still on her feet?"

Charlie Dick nodded. "She was when we put her in the barn."

At that moment Miriam and Kathleen came into the room. "I told you not to wake up Grandpa for any of your old teases," Miriam insisted. "And I'm going to tell Mama on you for doing it."

Grandpa narrowed his eyes. "You ain't up to one of your tricks?"

"Oh, no. Buttons looked real bad."

"There's only one thing to do if she's on her side." Grandpa angrily tugged at the sheet over him as though it were a chain that bound him to the bed. "Most you can save, but some you can't. Anna, bring your ma's butcher knife here so I can show Charlie Dick what to do."

As Anna left, the solemnity of the situation hit Charlie Dick. "You mean *I* gotta stick a cow?" he asked, his eyes large.

"Who else?" Grandpa asked rather crossly. "You can do it, can't you?"

Charlie Dick wiggled his bare toes nervously on the floor. "I guess I can, but it sure won't be no fun."

"It's no fun just standing by doing nothing watching a cow die neither. And your pa can't afford to lose a cow now."

Anna came back with the knife. Kathleen started to bawl, but when Grandpa jerked his head at her in a frown, she muffled the noise with a hand. Grandpa took the butcher knife and slid his finger over the point. Reflected light skipped up its narrow blade.

"Now here's what you do . . ."

Charlie Dick stared at the hard steel while Grandpa measured his hand span with his grandson's. He kept an ear cocked hopefully for the sound of the pickup motor as the old man explained how to measure his hand spans on the cow to find the exact right spot to make the hole to let the gases escape. His weary ancient body had some of its old energy for a moment as he spiritedly explained the

126

task to Charlie Dick. "Now you repeat the directions," Grandpa ordered.

"One and a half of my hand spans, 'cause they're smaller than yours, from the left hipbone and one and a half hand spans down from the backbone."

"I want Mama," Kathleen sniffled.

Miriam had become very wide-eyed and quiet.

Grandpa continued. "Now if the cow's on her feet, you can risk sending one of the girls over after your pa. But if she's down, you better take care of it." He reached out, turned Charlie Dick around by the arm, and swatted him on the seat. "Go on now, and when you get back, I'll tell you about the time I went bear hunting up on Bald Mountain with your Uncle Henry and chained up that old black bear we used to have."

The girls followed as Charlie Dick marched from the bedroom into the kitchen.

"You stay here, Anna. You don't need to come," Charlie Dick said. Then his voice rose in annoyance. "And you stay here too, Kathleen. We don't need your crying going on."

"I want Mama," Kathleen howled when Charlie Dick and Miriam left the house.

As they approached the barn, Charlie Dick swung the butcher knife jauntily at his side like a stick to lighten the burden that was pressing on him. Buttons will be on her feet, he assured himself, and she'll look just fine. He refused to allow himself to glance toward the lane, which the pickup would use in coming back from town, but he noticed Miriam's head craned in that direction.

"If you've been teasing us, Charlie Dick. . ." she threatened to cover her nervousness.

He pushed the barn door partly open and gazed into the dimness. He stood there so long that Miriam crowded beside him and peered around the door frame. The cow lay on her side, her middle swollen and her legs out stiff before her. The silence was so deep that Charlie Dick wondered whether she was breathing.

"I'm scared," Miriam whispered.

"I can't see as how there's anything to be scared of." Charlie Dick made his voice tough, not unlike Walt's, to bolster himself up, then pushed the door the rest of the way open. The sunshine spilled into the barn and across the cow's face, where the glazed eyes seemed not to register its brightness.

After Mama came back from White City, she drove immediately over to the east field in the pickup and brought Daddy. Charlie Dick went into the barn with them, but the girls stayed outside. As he walked near the cow, the smell of blood and partly digested alfalfa from the cow's side struck his nostrils, and he wanted to turn and run from the barn as he had when he finished the job earlier. Instead he asked, "How is she, Dad?"

The silence as his father bent over the cow was broken only by the buzzing of a big horse fly. Dad moved up near

Buttons' head and squatted there a moment before he replied.

"I guess she's gone."

"Gone? But she can't be. Are you sure?" He ran to Dad's side.

"Come on, Charlie Dick, we might as well go." Mama put her arm around his shoulder.

But Charlie Dick pulled away and bent over Buttons. She was dead all right. Even he could tell that. As he walked out of the barn, he struggled to keep back the tears. When he saw his sisters standing by at the watering trough and staring, he stuck out his jaw, broke away from Mama's arm, and ran off.

The rough rafter of the granary pressed uncomfortably into Charlie Dick's stomach as he lay face down, peering over it into the bin. The shining sides of the sheet metal gleamed from a ray of the evening sun that came through a knothole and shone on the little that was left of last year's red wheat in the bin. In the fall when it was full to the top Charlie Dick had jumped from the rafter and sunk into the red kernels all the way to his thighs. When he pulled his legs out, the cuffs of his pants had been full of wheat and his legs had felt heavy when he tried to walk. But now he only stared unseeing at the remaining wheat in the dimness below him.

"Charlie Dick," he heard Kathleen call from somewhere in the barnyard.

"Dick," Elizabeth Eliza's voice echoed.

Charlie Dick lifted his head, but he didn't answer. His nose began to run again, and he wiped it with his sleeve. He relaxed when he heard them call from farther away. He wished they would stop looking for him. They didn't need him now Mama was back, and if he went to the house, his sisters would stare at him in their pitying way, as they had earlier, and make it hard to keep from crying. He gritted his teeth in defiance. What use had it been to try to save the cow with the butcher knife when she had only died anyway? It had been so hard to do and no fun at all. His stomach churned as he remembered forcing the knife through the white hide.

"Charlie Dick," Kathleen was now near the granary.

"Dick," Elizabeth Eliza copied.

Kathleen's voice rose as she added, "Grandpa wants you. And he says if you don't come in right away, he'll wallop you good when you do come."

Charlie Dick sat up. That was different if Grandpa wanted him instead of all those pitying females. When he heard Kathleen's voice calling on the other side of the barnyard, he crawled along the rafter to the wall and swung himself down. He wiped at his nose and eyes with his shirt tail before he stepped from the granary. He took the back way to the house and headed straight to Grandpa's room.

Charlie Dick stepped close to the bed, but Charles Hale didn't look up even though his eyes were open. Grandpa lay without noticing him for so long that Charlie Dick cleared his throat. When that didn't bring any response, he asked softly, "Did you want me, Grandpa?"

Finally the old man looked at him. Charlie Dick was surprised at the cold look in his eyes.

"You sure don't practice what you preach, do you?" old Charles Hale accused the boy.

"I don't know," Charlie Dick replied, startled because instead of a scolding he had expected some comfort.

"Well, I do. If the cow had got better, you would have been dancing on one toe on the top of the barn and crowing to the world, but instead you made a face at your sisters and ran away and hid."

"That don't have nothing to do with me not doing what I say." Charlie Dick scowled down at his grandfather, wondering if the old man had gone sour like he was when he first came to the Hale house.

"It sure does. Just 'cause the cow died doesn't mean you didn't do a brave thing—a good thing too. Your pa said he couldn't have done more himself."

A tear slid from Charlie Dick's eyes, but Grandpa didn't seem to notice.

"And you're letting a bad thing that happened make you forget the good thing you done. And that's just what you told me not to do one day."

"I did?" Charlie Dick wiped the tear off his cheek and screwed up his face trying to remember ever saying anything like that, but the idea seemed new to him. "I don't think I ever said that."

"Yup, you did." The old man nodded and plopped his

lips together with assurance. "You told me I shouldn't lay here being cross and bitter 'cause I'm in a bad way now, because I got to do so many exciting things in the past. That's what you said."

"That don't seem the same to me." Charlie Dick tilted his head to one side trying to compare himself to Grandpa.

"It's just the same."

"Well, maybe," Charlie Dick conceded.

"It sure is, and I figured it was pretty good advice—to cherish the good and forget the bad—even coming from a ten-year-old. So I done it, a little anyway, and it made me feel better."

Charlie Dick looked at the white hair on the pillow. "I guess it makes me feel better too," he admitted.

"Then pull up that chair and I'll tell you about the time we chained up that bear on Bald Mountain like I promised you."

Charlie Dick was aware that Grandpa in his own way had given him the comfort he needed. He slid the wooden chair up close to the bed, but he paused without sitting down, listening to some distant sound.

"Maybe I'd better run and tell Kathleen where I am. She's still hollering her head off for me down in the barn-yard."

9

Dad spoke to him man to man, not commanding, but appealing. "With your mother out helping me, it's the only way I can think to work it out today, Charlie Dick. Miriam can handle things pretty well, but still in case anything should go wrong, it's nice for me to know you're close by to take care of it." They were at the flowing well, Dad on his way back to work after dinner.

Even though he would rather have taken a shovel to the field, Charlie Dick realized that today, because of the fire, he was needed at the house. What would Miriam have done when Buttons bloated, for instance, without Charlie Dick?

"Anna and Kathleen have to have someone with them when they work, so if you stay here and help them do the dishes and take the clothes in off the lines and fold them, I mean really get some work done, then Miriam can get

Elizabeth Eliza down for her nap so she can sit by Grandpa. He doesn't seem to be as well today, and I want her to stay with him."

"But I *would* like to go to town with Walt later," Charlie Dick said. Today, Founders' Day, he would get Anna's doll, the right way, with the money Walt had promised to pay him.

"We should have a good fire line before then, so Mama can come back to the house. Yes, I think it will be all right. You come over to the field after the work's done —around three o'clock. Walt should be able to go then. Will those arrangements suit you?"

"That suits me fine," Charlie Dick grinned.

His Dad clapped him on the shoulder before he headed for the field. Charlie Dick watched him go toward the clouds of smoke that rose on the north side of the farm —the fence line that Dad had a hard time keeping up between the Hale and the Rupert farms.

It had been the urgency of the fire that had disturbed the scheduled work and the plans for a longer trip to town.

"I don't see how he thinks a fire around his field is going to get rid of the crickets," Mama had complained at dinner when she got up to refill the gravy bowl, "not unless he plans to keep it going all summer."

"You know Jack Rupert. He does everything in spurts. Today he's going to rid himself of all the crickets—so the fire. Tomorrow they'll move in again and he won't lift a finger against 'em," Dad replied as he speared some green beans with his fork.

"It seems downright dangerous to me," Walt said, "to build a big fire that close to somebody else's property. If a wind came up . . ."

"Rupert doesn't have any responsibility about other people's property, nor for his own, for that matter. In the spring he's the last one in the whole valley to get his crops in, and his animals are always out roaming around other people's farms and causing mischief. You ought to buy that land, Walt. You could get it for a song 'cause the place is so run down. You're a good worker, and you'd have it in shape within a year."

Interest lit Walt's eyes. "You think I could make it?" But then the spark died, and he shook his head. "No, I don't suppose it would work out for me."

"Did much wheat burn where his fire broke through into our field?" Mama asked.

"No," Dad assured her, "not worth worrying about. Walt and I put it right out. What I hate, though, is missing a day's work because of standing guard against the fire along our whole fence line."

But a breeze was rustling the leaves of the cottonwoods when the men were through with dinner.

"Maybe you'd better come over and help us, Margaret," Dad had decided. "We'll get a plow down there. The horses might be skittish that near a fire or else Charlie Dick could do it. If we clear a strip near the fence, that'll put us out of danger so Walt can run into Hanging Rock for a couple of hours and see his friend."

Despite Charlie Dick's good intentions to do what his father asked, the afternoon started out to be almost intolerable. Kathleen refused to do a thing Charlie Dick told her.

"I'm going to wash the dishes," he said as he poured hot water from the tea kettle into the big dishpan, "and you can help Anna wipe, Kathleen."

"I want to wash," Kathleen said. She hadn't helped stack the dishes and now she was sprawled on the bench at the table.

"You'd just play in the water. We don't want to be all afternoon doing dishes. You help Anna wipe."

"I don't want to." She began to sniffle.

"Well, you have to."

Kathleen howled her loudest.

Running steps were heard on the stairs, and Miriam burst into the kitchen.

"Charlie Dick, you stop making Kathleen cry. I had Elizabeth Eliza almost asleep and now she's wide awake again. If you don't stop teasing Kathleen, I'll tell Mama."

"I wasn't teasing her at all." Charlie Dick kept his voice even because he remembered that Miriam, who wanted to go to town today too, was not going to be able to.

Without listening, Miriam stormed out of the room and up the stairs again.

Charlie Dick was tempted to tell Kathleen what a crybaby he thought she was and to "smile" at her in his particular way, but he refrained.

"We don't need you at all, Kathleen," he said as he placed the dishes in the water. "We can do just fine without you—Anna and me can." He winked at Anna.

Anna had only started to wipe when Kathleen sidled up between her and Charlie Dick with a dish towel in hand. Charlie Dick ignored her until she had finished wiping her first plate. Then he gave her a clean cup to wipe and a proper smile at the same time. She smiled back as she stuffed the end of the towel down inside the cup.

She even helped them carry the clothes from the lines after the dishes were done. When they were finished folding the clothes, Charlie Dick told Anna loudly so Kathleen could hear, "I didn't know six-year-olds could work so hard."

Delighted, Kathleen skipped off to Grandpa's bedroom to be with Miriam for awhile.

So at last it was almost three o'clock, and Charlie Dick, his work done, left the house for the fields to find Walt. Anna was at his side. When they walked through the pasture, they could see Mama on the plow driving the team in front of the billowing clouds of gray smoke.

"Do you see Walt? I don't see him."

Anna's hair fluttered with a gust of wind. She stepped around a prairie dog mound, her eyes searching the smoke bank.

"Maybe he's over there with Daddy."

She pointed to the far side of the wheat field. John Hale worked with a shovel on the side of the roadway where the fire had spread, trying to stop it from flanking the farm on the west.

"I don't see Walt by the road, but the pickup is at the end of the pasture. Maybe he's down there."

When they crossed the creek, Charlie Dick saw Walt working with a shovel near the fence in a patch of young willows. Now that he knew where the big man was, he could relax until it was time for them to go.

"I know, Anna, let's play in the trees. We've worked hard. We deserve to play for a few minutes."

His sister followed him through a tangle of willows. They came out in a small clearing where a huge old cottonwood with spreading branches grew. It was one of Charlie Dick's favorite climbing trees on the creek. He lifted his foot to the lowest branch and sprang onto the limb.

"Come on, Anna," he said, "we can see over the whole farm from the top of this tree."

With assurance he climbed hand over hand. When he looked down, Anna was sitting on the lowest branch with her small face turned up to him.

"Come on, Anna. You can see everything from here. You can see the house and the barns and the creek going down the whole valley, and you can see the place where the fire is burning."

Charlie Dick looked along the fire line. Dad worked feverishly on the roadside farther down from where he had previously been. Somehow the fire had spread past him. The dust from Mama's plow was mingling with the smoke from the fire and blowing over the wheat field. Sometimes the smoke almost hid her from view.

"Gee, Anna, you should see how high those flames are leaping over there in Mr. Rupert's field. Come and see."

But Anna didn't move.

"You've got to see this."

"I don't want to climb that high," she said mildly.

Anna always was afraid of everything. Of course she couldn't come up by herself.

"I'll help you. It's sure a mighty sight." He climbed down, swinging from branch to branch. "It's like being on top of the whole world. It'll be fun, Anna. I'll help you, and I won't let you get hurt neither."

He pulled her to her feet on the limb and gave her a boost as she fearfully grasped the branch above. It was a struggle to lift her, for she was as limp as a sack of corn-meal. A sharp twig scratched her leg, but she didn't complain, and her lips, already pressed into a tight line, didn't change. Puffing, Charlie Dick finally had her high in the tree.

"There, see Anna, ain't it worth it?" he asked as he helped her sit down on a rather spindly limb.

But immediately Charlie Dick knew that bringing her up had been a mistake. The little girl twined her arms around the trunk and riveted her eyes to the mountains in the distance. "Don't you worry, Anna. I'll help you right down again." Then he suddenly exclaimed, "Look how high the fire is now!"

As he watched, he marveled that the fire had doubled in size in just the time he had been helping Anna. The tree swayed. Anna's long hair blew out behind her. She closed her eyes.

"I guess it's the wind that's fanning the fire."

Charlie Dick kept hold of Anna's arm to keep her from being so frightened as he scanned the fire line. Suddenly the flames in one place swept across the plowed swath. He shaded his eyes, looking for his parents. His mother, apparently unaware that the fire had jumped into the grain, was working with the team on the far side of the field.

"Did you see that, Anna? I'd better run and tell Mama to plow out around that new fire."

He started to slide down through the branches but paused and looked back up at his little sister clinging above. Charlie Dick felt impatient with himself for taking her up there. And there wasn't time to help her down now. The grain would be burned up by the time he inched her all the way down.

"Anna, you know I've got to go or else I wouldn't leave you. I'll be right back as soon as I tell Mama. You stay there and don't move."

He leaped from the bottom limb to the ground and pushed out of the thick willows. Ducking under the fence, he raced through the wheat. The wind blew harder, and the smoke pouring over the wheat field grew thicker. He felt the heat from the fire and decided that he was near the place the flames had jumped the swath. He swerved out into the wheat, but the stifling smoke followed him. After stopping for a second to get his bearings, he again rushed on. The gusty wind tossed his hair down over his eyes and the smoke scorched his throat. Everything had looked so plain from up in the tree, but now down in the smoke, he was confused and lost. He gave up trying to reach Mama and turned and ran with the gale.

It seemed an eternity before he hit a clear stream of flowing air. He was surprised to find himself near the center of the field. Tongues of flame leaped high into the air near him and clouds of black spread over the field. Smoke poured from the willows in the pasture. Abruptly he drew in his breath, for even as he watched, the fire jumped toward the creek.

Anna!

Charlie Dick suddenly shot forward as he thought of his little sister clinging high in the tree he could no longer see. Once his toes slipped when some dry clods crumbled under them, and he sprawled into the wheat mashing it down. He sprang to his feet and ran on. The fire moved faster, however, forcing him to detour into the pasture. He dashed toward the cottonwood tree, but his heart sank, for the willows along the whole creek seemed afire. In a frenzy he ran to the edge of the burning willows.

"Anna! Anna!" he screamed into the flames.

He swung toward the creek, splashed up it, and vaulted to the bank near the big tree.

"Anna," he called as he spied her silhouette dark against the billowing smoke.

Madly he clawed his way up the trunk. The tree swayed fearfully as he reached her. Anna's eyes were firmly shut. Her arms hugged the trunk.

"Come on, Anna. I'll help you down." He jerked her arm, but she clung tightly. "Anna, we ain't got time for any nonsense. Open your eyes." He tried to pry her hands form the wood. "Hang on to me, Anna. Let go of the tree."

Anna's knuckles were white.

"If you don't come down, I won't never play with you again."

Smoke poured from nearby bushes and blew across the trunk of their cottonwood. For a moment Charlie Dick could not see the ground.

"And I won't get you a doll like I promised neither."

He worked one hand loose, but as he pulled on the other, the first again grasped the branch. Charlie Dick looked around frantically. From the gray smoke streams across the creek, a dark, denim-clad figure suddenly emerged.

"Walt," Charlie Dick shouted.

The roaring wind-fanned fire swallowed his call. On the run, the big man headed for the pickup.

Charlie Dick crashed down through the branches.

Halfway he abandoned the tree and leaped. He rushed through the creek and along the other bank.

With lungs bursting, he dodged some burning grass and emerged from the smoke. Ahead Walt was jerking open the pickup door. Somehow Charlie Dick forced a new burst of speed. He whizzed over the tall grass of the pasture.

"Walt," he screamed. The sound of the pickup motor starting drowned out his voice.

Before Charlie Dick reached the truck, the wheels started rolling. In a last desperate effort Charlie Dick sprang toward the moving pickup. The metal door clanked loudly as he slammed into it. He clawed wildly for a hand hold, but missed the edge of the window and tumbled from the running board. The rear wheel of the truck stopped only inches from his side.

"What the heck are you doing?" Walt's head was out the window.

Charlie Dick rolled from under the truck and jumped to his feet.

"Get in here quick," Walt commanded.

"You've got to help . . ." Charlie Dick began breathlessly.

"But the big man reached out the window and grabbed Charlie Dick by the collar. "Cut the talk and get in."

Charlie Dick tried to tug himself free. "Anna," he puffed. "We've got to get Anna first."

Walt let go of his shirt. "What do you mean, Anna? Where's Anna?"

"In a tree, and I can't get her down. You've gotta help me," Charlie Dick pleaded.

The pickup lurched as Walt let out the clutch and then jumped out.

"Show me where she is."

He half dragged Charlie Dick back toward the trees. When the boy got his feet under him, they ran together into the smoke. At the creek Charlie Dick waded in front to find the way.

"Here," he yelled to Walt.

He jumped onto the bank and scrambled through the heat. Already the branches on the far side of the big tree were smoking. Walt pushed in front of him and climbed into the tree.

"Get back to the creek. If I'm not there in a minute, don't stop running until you get to the house." When Charlie Dick didn't move, the big man broke off a branch and threw it at him. "Go on."

It hit Charlie Dick on the shoulder, but he stared a moment longer before he turned and bolted to the stream. He stood shin-deep in water. The nearby grass burst into flames and melted away into a black void. The heat was intense. Charlie Dick splashed water over himself, his face contorted with agonized waiting.

With a ripping noise in the bushes a large body came flying through the fire into the creek. The water hissed as

144

Walt fell to his knees. Anna's tiny body was pressed tightly to his chest. One of her hands was twined in his collar and the other still held a fragment of a branch of the tree.

As Walt bent over patting water on the burning hem of Anna's dress, Charlie Dick saw fire smoldering on the back of his shirt and splashed water toward him.

Walt leaped to his feet. "Let's get out of here," he roared as fiercely as the flames around him.

They ran coughing through the smoke. When they neared the pickup, fire still poured from the big man's shirt. Walt paused at the pickup door, and Charlie Dick showered his back with handfuls of loose dirt.

The next instant they were all in the pickup as it bounced over the rough meadow ground.

Charlie Dick sank back onto the cool seat next to Anna, and when the pickup jolted suddenly, a sob bounced involuntarily out of him. He glanced at Walt, hoping the hired man hadn't heard him cry like a girl.

But he had no need to worry. One tear was making a small white path from the corner of Walt's eye down his smoke-blackened face.

10

The house was still. Even the faraway sound of Elizabeth Eliza's crying in the upstairs bedroom had now quieted. As Charlie Dick sat on his cot alone in the porch, he wondered why even the usual creaking sounds of the old house were silent. Not even a tiny breeze played along the eaves to send out hollow whispers to break the mood.

Although no one spoke about it, the waiting silence seemed to come from the closed door of Grandpa's room, where Dad had gone in to sit after he and Charlie Dick had done only the very most necessary chores.

"Charlie Dick's so quiet," Miriam had observed at dinner a little earlier, "he must be thinking up some mean trick."

But Charlie Dick hadn't been then, nor was he now. Miriam had even accused him of having caused the terrible smell in the chicken coop that morning, but a skunk had been there, and he had nothing to do with it.

The fact was he didn't feel like playing tricks. Part of the feeling came from the dreadful expectancy that filled the house, and part came from Charlie Dick's heavy burden of guilt over Walt, who lay on his stomach on a real bed in the living room, his burned back bare and oozing. In the two days since the fire, Charlie Dick had not spoken to the big man. How do you say thank you to someone you've hardly ever spoken kindly to before? Do you say, "Nice weather we're having, and by the way thank you for saving my sister's life." The thought of Anna clinging to the tree in the smoke made his stomach churn. What if he had succeeded with his tricks in driving Walt away from the farm? "Oh, yes, and I'm sorry I played all those mean tricks on you all summer."

Anna, her eyes down, came slowly through the yard. She walked listlessly into the porch and without looking up sat down on the cot next to Charlie Dick.

"What have you been doing?" Charlie Dick questioned to encourage the forlorn little figure to speak.

"Just walking around," she answered. Then she looked at him. Her eyes were full of anxiety. "Will Walt be all right?" she asked.

"Oh, sure Anna. You don't need to worry about that."

She looked down at her small hands in her lap. "It's all my fault."

Just this once Charlie Dick wished she were more like one of her sisters and would bawl at him like Kathleen,

"You did it, Charlie Dick," or yell at him like Miriam, "You got me up in that tree, Charlie Dick, and I'll tell Mama." But the dark eyes held no accusation.

"No, Anna." He shook his head over and over again. "No. No. I got you up in that tree. It's my fault, and don't you even think about it again."

The worry lines around Anna's eyes began to ease.

"In fact, I was just thinking to myself how I was going to go in to see Walt and tell him how everything happened and tell him that I'm sorry he burned his back doing this good thing for us. Would that make you feel better, Anna? And I'll tell him thanks for you too if you want." Charlie Dick stood up.

Anna nodded. Her eyes shone with gratitude.

Charlie Dick left the porch. He knew, however, that words would not be enough to ease his conscience. They would be a start, but he would need more than words to make up to the hired man for all the mean tricks he had pulled on him.

In the living room Walt lay on his stomach, a sheet pulled up only to his waist. Above it his bare back was crusted, oozing in spots. His eyes were closed, so Charlie Dick sat down in the rocking chair and began tapping his foot. In case the big man did wake up, Charlie Dick would appear relaxed and inconspicuous.

Walt did not stir, and shortly Charlie Dick heard the sound of a car in the lane. Mama came into the living room.

"That must be Dr. Ryan," she said. "He told us he'd

come back out today." She went outside to meet the doctor on the steps.

"Yes, I'll look at John's Dad while I'm here," Dr. Ryan said to Mama as they came into the house together. "And I stopped by the Bensen's with the note you sent for Walt's friend, Mrs. Hale. How are you today, Walt?" he heartily greeted his patient when he reached the bed. "Say, you're looking better already."

"He does look better," Mama agreed.

Walt turned his head on the pillow and grinned. "I don't feel so bad any more either."

As he bent over Walt, Dr. Ryan continued, "I stopped by with the note Mrs. Hale sent for your friend, but Bill Bensen said he left a couple of days ago without giving notice and didn't come back. Bill wasn't too happy because now is the time he needs help the most. I asked around and no one seems to know where he went.

"I'll bet he's working for . . ." Charlie Dick started to say.

But Dr. Ryan continued talking, anxious to tell the town gossip.

"There's a big stir in town, and Old Stone is in the middle of it, storming around and making everybody mad at him as usual. Someone broke into his house while he was giving his big speech at the Founders' Day Program. His mattress was ripped up, and he found his desk pried open and three hundred dollars gone."

"Mr. Stone?" Charlie Dick asked.

The grownups, engrossed in their own conversation, ignored him. "Stone figured some boys did it just for meanness," Dr. Ryan said. "The sheriff, though, says it looks like a pro job, the way the lock on the desk was jimmied. But Stone says he better find the boys who did it and lock them up no matter who their parents are. Apparently one of them came nosing around supposedly to ask for a job and cased out his house."

"I suppose it was liable to happen sooner or later," Mama said, "with the ridiculous rumors always about of how he keeps his money around the house, in his mattress and such."

Suddenly Charlie Dick sat bolt upright. His mouth fell open as he stared across the living room without seeing a thing.

Could it be possible? Yet it must be so. Alf had stolen that money. But worse, Walt had been going to town on Founders' Day to help him. Walt was a crook!

Charlie Dick realized that Dr. Ryan had gone into the bedroom to see Grandpa. The boy stood up and walked to the front door. Without looking, he knew Walt's eyes were on him. He casually opened the screen and stepped outside. He was standing by the car when the doctor came from the house.

"Dr. Ryan," Charlie Dick said as the man approached.

"Yes?" the doctor asked as he walked around Charlie Dick to the door.

"Maybe I ought to have you give the sheriff a message for me."

"I guess you know who broke into Stone's?" the doctor joked. He placed his bag inside on the seat.

"I sure do."

"Then who?" The doctor's face was jovial.

Charlie Dick stood silent. If he told why he knew Alf was the thief, he would implicate Walt. He couldn't tell on Walt now—not after he'd saved Anna. He couldn't and he wouldn't. That is how he would make it up to Walt for all the tormenting. Quickly Charlie Dick searched for an answer to the doctor.

"The man in the moon," he laughed and slapped his knee, pretending it was a big joke.

The doctor gave a weak smile as he stepped into his car. He obviously thought it wasn't funny.

As he returned to the house, Charlie Dick reflected that this incriminating knowledge about Walt was just what he had wanted a few days ago to send the big man— his enemy—on his way. But now things had changed.

Afraid to break the mood of the day, Charlie Dick quietly entered the house. He tiptoed over to the bed and bent down near Walt's face. The hired man's eyes opened for a moment then closed again.

"Walt," Charlie Dick whispered, "if you're awake, maybe I'll keep you company for a minute."

Walt stirred, then pulled himself up on his elbows and looked at Charlie Dick with anticipation, but he didn't say anything.

"You're a hero." Charlie Dick hesitated self-consciously, for he had never spoken so openly to the big man before. "Saving Anna, I mean." he continued. "Poor little Anna. She's always afraid of everything. It was me that got her up in that tree."

"I guess we all knew that Anna wouldn't have climbed the tree herself."

"Then how come nobody's mad about it?"

"That's just one of those things that happen, Charlie Dick. You couldn't have known the fire would suddenly come that way."

Because of Walt's understanding, Charlie Dick found it wasn't so hard to say what he'd come for.

"Anyway, I'm sure grateful to you, and she is too. We're awful sorry you burned your back."

"It's not burned so bad it won't get better, so don't sweat over it," Walt said.

"But I'm not sorry you missed your trip into Hanging Rock on Founders' Day to see Alf. I'm not sorry because I wouldn't want you to be gone off like Alf, nor in trouble neither. And you would have been without the fire to stop you, wouldn't you?"

"Yes," Walt admitted.

"You don't need to worry. I won't tell nothing I know. You don't need to pay me the two dollars neither. And I won't tease you any more and I won't play any more tricks on you unless it's just for fun. I used to bother you because I didn't like you. But I guess it's not right to pull tricks just to be mean."

Walt relaxed back onto the pillow. "Maybe I wasn't so nice to you either."

154

"That's O.K." Charlie Dick began to feel good.

"But you mean you won't tell anybody about me and Alf sending you to Old Stone's place?" Walt thoughtfully asked.

"That's right. I won't tell a single soul."

"Don't you think you ought to tell your dad?"

Charlie Dick was perplexed. He had expected Walt to be grateful. "It don't seem right to tell on someone who's done such a good thing for you."

"But your pa would want to know. I think a lot of your pa. And I've been lying here for two days thinking how good it is that I didn't meet Alf at Stone's place like he wanted me to and run off with him chasing a rainbow all the way to Alaska. I'm glad I'm still here."

"I'm glad too."

"That's what I mean. It's been kind of nice having your family all fussing over me and knowing they're glad I'm here and all right. And not just because of Anna either. That's why I think you ought to tell your pa what you know about the Stone job."

"I don't see how that would do any good," Charlie Dick argued, remembering how harsh his dad had been over the stolen spurs.

"You see," Walt explained, "he's willing to get me started on the Rupert farm. I know he'll help me any way he can. But first I've got a year and a half prison term to finish up."

"A prison term?"

"Yes."

Of course, a crook would have a prison term. "I sure feel terrible about that."

"Me too," Walt said, "but I never felt more like a man than I have this summer. I want to work my own way in this world, and I want to be free. I like this country and the Rupert farm would be just perfect for me. But I guess I've got to take care of that time so I can quit running long enough to harvest something I plant."

"I sure feel terrible," Charlie Dick repeated.

"Go get your pa and send him in here so I can talk to him about it before I chicken out and ruin the last part of my life like I did the first."

When Charlie Dick remained, unwilling to go, Walt ordered again. "Go on, now."

Charlie Dick turned and walked reluctantly toward Grandpa's room. There was nothing he could do for Walt after all. How could anyone help in trouble like Walt had?

Charlie Dick opened the bedroom door. Dad was sitting on a chair by Grandpa's bed with his head in his hands.

Because Grandpa was asleep, Charlie Dick walked close to his father and whispered. "Walt wants to talk to you for a minute."

Dad glanced at the old man in the bed. "But I'm sitting with Grandpa right now. Maybe a little later."

Either Mama or Dad had been with Grandpa night and day for the past twenty-four hours, and none of the children had been assigned to his room.

"But Walt needs you real bad right now. He's got something important to tell you. I'll sit with Grandpa while you go out there."

His father looked long into his eyes, and Charlie Dick wondered if Dad was remembering how his son had hated to be with Grandpa at the beginning of summer.

"Grandpa and me are good friends. I don't mind sitting with him."

John Hale slowly stood up. As Charlie Dick slid onto the chair in his place, his dad rested his hand on his back.

"I won't be long."

After a last look at Grandpa, he turned and left the room.

Dad had only been gone for a moment when Grandpa mumbled shortly. Talking in his sleep, Charlie Dick decided, for the old eyes, half open, had an unseeing, sleepy quality about them. He did wish the old man would wake up so he could tell him about Walt, but Grandpa only began muttering again. Charlie Dick couldn't understand what he was saying, but on impulse he reached over and touched the wrinkled hand that was resting on his chest.

Grandpa's eyelids lifted all the way open. Charlie Dick stood up and bent over him smiling.

"Hi, Grandpa," he said brightly.

Grandpa blinked as though trying to focus his eyes. "Well, Charlie Dick," he said, his voice thin and weak. "You're like a ray of sunshine after all those sad-faced people sitting around here."

"I don't mind being here," Charlie Dick said. "In fact I've got lots to tell you."

"A ray of sunshine . . ." The old man seemed trapped in his own line of thought. "It's a gift, cheerfulness is. A mighty good gift." The voice faded, and Charlie Dick had to lean closer to hear. "Use it to make things easier for them around you—not harder. Will you, Charlie Dick?"

"Yes, I will, Grandpa. I promise." Charlie Dick meant it. He'd never make it harder for anyone again like he had for Walt.

"Not harder," Grandpa repeated.

Charlie Dick didn't like the way Grandpa's voice had become slower, like a record running down. "I sure will, Grandpa. In fact that's what I want to talk to you about. You know Walt. I sure didn't like him at first, and I did mean things to him, but he did this good thing. He saved Anna, and now I'm sorry for the tricks I pulled, and I want to do something good for him. But he has to go back to prison, and . . ."

Grandpa's eyes were shut again and his breath was coming hard through his partly open mouth. Charlie Dick was suddenly frightened.

Then the door opened and Dad was standing beside him. "Has he been awake?"

Charlie Dick had to swallow before he answered. "For a minute. And he said some nice things to me."

Suddenly Charlie Dick swung his face up and looked straight at his father. "He'll get better, won't he?"

John Hale didn't answer. When his rough hand went about Charlie Dick's shoulder and caressed it gently, his eyes were as filmy as a net curtain.

11

The funeral had been nice. That's what everybody said. Charlie Dick had heard many people tell Dad so, and Dan Barns's father came up to Charlie Dick himself outside the church in Hanging Rock afterward.

"That was a nice funeral for your Grandpa, Charlie Dick," he said. "He lived a long time and was one of the strong ones in the valley. A fine man he was."

Charlie Dick thanked him politely, but he didn't smile.

When Dan said, "School starts in only a month and then we can see each other every day," Charlie Dick replied vacantly, "Uh-huh, that will be fun," as he fingered the huge black pocketknife that weighed his Sunday pants down lopsided. But he hadn't shown the knife to Dan.

Now Charlie Dick took the big knife out of his pocket. He sat alone in the pickup in front of the Hale house, waiting for Walt to change from the vest and pants

160

which Dad had borrowed for him to wear to Grandpa's funeral. Slowly he turned the knife over, feeling its hard, rough sides. He opened all the blades one at a time, then folded them back shut again.

It sure was nice of Grandpa to give him his big five-blade pocketknife. Actually Grandpa hadn't given it to Charlie Dick. Aunt Rosey had found it among Grandpa's possessions that were stored at her house and given it to Charlie Dick at the funeral. "He told me he wanted you to have this," she had said.

Charlie Dick brushed angrily at a tear on his cheek. He had managed to keep from crying at the funeral while Miriam next to him on the bench shook with sobs. He knew that Grandpa himself wouldn't have been a bit sad about having died. Still Charlie Dick could not bear to think of life at the Hale house with Grandpa gone.

Walt, wearing his own clothes again, came out of the house. Charlie Dick slipped the knife back in his pocket and watched the big man walk slowly toward the pickup, looking sideways longingly in the direction of the Rupert farm. As he neared the truck, Charlie Dick called out the window to him, "Daddy just ran down to the barn to turn some water into the trough for the calves. He forgot to this morning with all the goings-on. He said to tell you he'd be right back."

Walt nodded and leaned against the pickup.

Charlie Dick could understand why he was in no hurry for Dad to drive him into town to the sheriff's office,

even though it was Walt's own idea. A year and a half was a long time.

Charlie Dick cleared his throat. "I'm sorry you have to go, Walt."

"I hate to go, too."

"I don't want you to go because I'm afraid you won't come back." Charlie Dick's voice trembled. "And I'll never see you again—like Grandpa."

"No, I'll be back." Walt sounded certain.

But still Charlie Dick wanted to make sure. "You promise, Scout's honor, cross your heart and hope to die if you should ever tell a lie . . ."

Walt turned and laughed softly. "I can't promise like that. You never know what will happen. I'm sure planning to be back. But three weeks ago I never thought I'd hear you talking like that." He grinned at the boy, jesting.

"Me too." Charlie Dick managed a little smile.

No, he had not expected to be sorry when Walt left, not after all his scheming to get rid of Walt so that Dad would pay him wages afterward. Charlie Dick still planned to do Walt's share of the work as he had told Dad he would, but somehow now with the trouble of both Walt and Grandpa going, it didn't seem right to bother Dad about money.

As Dad came around the corner of the chicken coop, Mama and the girls emerged from the house. They reached the pickup before Dad and each had to give Walt a hug. All were talking at once.

Then Miriam said, "And we'll all write, and often too."

"I can write Kathleen," the six-year-old contributed. "I'll write to you too."

"Good."

"I'll remind them to write," Charlie Dick added when he got a chance.

In the midst of it all Miriam pushed Anna to the front. Charlie Dick was surprised that she was there at all, for he knew she hated good-byes as much as hellos. In the sudden silence Miriam poked her. But the prepared speech that Miriam was urging her to go on with would not come. With face flushed, she said stiffly, "Good-bye."

Walt ran his hand down her long hair. "Good-bye, little Anna."

Then Mama gave him a box of cookies the size of a bake pan. "It's a good thing for you to be going back, Walt," she said. "We'll all be waiting for you."

Charlie Dick looked away out the windshield of the pickup in case Walt was embarrassed by all the female show of emotion, but when he climbed stiffly into the seat by Charlie Dick, careful not to bump his sore back, he didn't seem at all embarrassed.

"I won't keep John in town long. I know he needs to get back for chores," Walt told Mama as he balanced the box of cookies on his lap. "He can just drop me off at the sheriff's."

Dad started the motor. "I'll stay a bit. I've got my two cents' worth to put in for you, you know."

164

"And I need to do some business. It'll just take me a minute," Charlie Dick announced.

But no one paid any attention to him. The girls and Mama waved as the pickup drove slowly out of the yard. They were still waving when it turned from the lane onto the main road.

12

That evening Anna hardly ate any supper although it was a regular feast—food the neighbors had showered on them because of the death in the family. Instead she aimlessly pushed a spoon through the potato salad as her eyes, bright with enchantment, looked down into her lap at the tiny doll. The golden hair of the doll was smoothed down carefully and the red dress flared out over Anna's fingers where she held the doll's legs.

"The deviled eggs are good, Anna," Mama prodded.

"Uh-huh," Anna agreed, but she didn't take a bite.

The words echoed hollowly in the big old house. Then the silence settled in again. Not even Elizabeth Eliza babbled. No one spoke, for what could be said about Grandpa's death, the thing that was foremost in everyone's mind. The girls ate quietly. Charlie Dick felt very tired.

"I guess you can be excused then, Anna, if you can't eat anything," Dad said.

166

Anna swung her legs over the bench and, stroking the doll's hair, slowly walked out of the kitchen.

"Miriam, you and Kathleen clear up these few dishes," Dad ordered. "Your mother needs to get Elizabeth Eliza to bed."

Still sitting at her place, Miriam began wearily stacking the plates. Slowly Kathleen pushed some cups together. Charlie Dick slid from the bench to leave the table.

"Just a minute, Charlie Dick," John Hale said. "There's something I need to ask you."

Charlie Dick turned to his father. "Yes?"

"I just want to know how you got that doll for Anna. It's a fine thing, but I just want to know how you got it."

"I'd rather not tell," Charlie Dick answered.

The girls stopped their work to listen.

John Hale considered for a moment. "I'd rather you did." He sounded tired.

"Well, you know Grandpa's big pocketknife. Aunt Rosey gave it to me today because Grandpa had said for me to have it."

His father nodded.

"So I sold it to Jake's Hardware this afternoon for two dollars and bought the doll at Bee's." Charlie Dick was glad Anna had left. He didn't want her to know.

"I see. I see." Dad nodded thoughtfully. "That was a fine thing to do, but do you think you ought to have sold a keepsake from Grandpa like that?"

Charlie Dick spread his arms out and shrugged.

"Maybe not. But you see I promised Anna, and anyway I don't need no pocketknife to remember Grandpa, but Anna needs her little doll."

Dad laid his hand on Charlie Dick's shoulder. "I guess you're right."

Mama looked tenderly at her son as she rocked Elizabeth Eliza on her lap.

The girls began again on the dishes. Miriam, at the stove with a stack of plates, said, "The water's cold and there isn't any wood in the box." Her shoulders sagged

wearily. She brought the dishes back to the table and set them down with a clank that echoed frustration like a shovel on stony ground. She blinked helplessly.

Kathleen picked up a crust of bread from a sandwich and began sadly gnawing on it. Her elbow touched a tin cup, knocking it off the edge of the table. Milk ran into a puddle under a chair. Everyone stared at it dejectedly.

Everything seemed hollow and worn out and useless. In the dim light Charlie Dick looked around the room at his family. Grandpa's weak voice echoed through his

mind. "Use it to make things easier." If he couldn't keep Grandpa's pocketknife, he could keep his words.

"I guess I can go out and get some wood," he said.

Everyone still stared at the milk.

"But if you hear me holler, open the door quick so I can get in before a old witch gets me." He forced a smile.

Everyone looked away from the milk and up at him.

"And I'll really come running fast if it's on its broomstick," Charlie Dick continued.

"Oh, Charlie Dick," Miriam scolded, but he was pleased to see she had enough spirit to pick up the plates again and set them in the empty dishpan.

Then Kathleen chuckled. Charlie Dick knew his act was a success, and he found it not so difficult to smile after all. He walked to the screen where a barn cat was peering in from the darkness, lifted her into his arms and carried her to the puddle of milk.

"There, this cat will clean up every drop of that milk for you. You watch her, Miriam. She'll lap it all up, even that little bit there with the ant floating in it." It was really only a speck of dirt.

"Ugh," Miriam said. Then with a smile she added, "Same old Charlie Dick."

"Same old Charlie Dick," Kathleen echoed.

"Same old Charlie Dick," repeated Mama affectionately.

About that everyone seemed warmly pleased.

"Well, almost," Dad said. He helped Mama to her feet and they walked from the kitchen.